URBANA FREE LIBRARY
S0-BCK-099

THE SKELLY MAN

Also by David Daniel

The Heaven Stone

The Tuesday Man

Ark

THE SKELLY MAN

DAVID DANIEL

ST. MARTIN'S PRESS
NEW YORK

Library of Congress Cataloging-in-Publication Data

Daniel, David.
The skelly man / David Daniel.
p. cm.
"A Thomas Dunne book".
ISBN 0-312-13602-1
I. Title.
PS3554.A5383S54 1995
813'.54—dc20 95-4901
CIP

First edition: September 1995

10 9 8 7 6 5 4 3 2 1

A special thanks to Louis Boxer, Ruth Cavin,
Dean Contover, Susan Crawford,
Joyce Rain Latora, Guy Lefebvre, Robert Sanchez,
Elisabeth Story, and Timothy Trask,
who were helpful in various ways.

This book is for Stephanie and Alexandra

THE SKELLY MAN

1

THE BRUINS HAD the power play going, but it didn't make a difference. When the clock ran out, it was the Leafs, 3–2, and Bobby Orr, when we needed him, was a pitchman for a Boston bank, golfing on worn-out knees. I signaled to Meg the bartender and told her a Molson's this time: Canada had earned it. Drinking from the bottle, I turned away from the TV behind the bar and gazed past the paper spiders and bats in the windows at the October night outside.

The mild air had brought fog, and the neon-stained city street was a colorized version of an old movie that looked better in black-and-white. But even the Lowell streets seemed cheerier than the late news. One downbeat story after another, then the highlights of the game I'd just watched. The lone good note was the weather: more Indian summer expected. I finished my beer. Coming up next, the broadcaster's voice informed me and the scattering of patrons in the Copper Kettle, was *The Good Night Show,* with host Jerry Corbin, and special guests I'd never heard of. I was ready to call it a wrap when Meg set another beer before me. I lifted my eyebrows.

"Gentleman down the bar," Meg said.

I looked and saw a tanned fellow, a little younger than I, who had come in between the story on the city's latest home invasion and robbery and the one about state auto-insurance rates going up again. He faked a smile, so I'd know it wasn't a pass, and gave the old minstrel-show wave. I lifted the bottle in thanks. He waited a full two swallows before he eased onto the bar stool at my left, planting cowboy boots in some exotic hide on the steel rail. He had on a gray twill suit, black shirt buttoned at the collar, and a bolo tie with a nugget of turquoise on it the size of a hockey puck. He was a fit forty with a smile full of caps that made the foam on my beer seem dingy. He hoisted a briefcase finished in the same hide as his boots onto the bar.

"Howdy," he said. "My name's Justin Ross."

If it was in my mental index, it was misfiled. But somebody buying you a beer this time of night was buying your ear. "Mine's Rasmussen," I said, taking his offered hand, which had powerful fingers studded with silver rings and more turquoise.

"Alex Rasmussen. I know. Meg tells me you're a private eye."

"She actually said that?"

"She might've used 'investigator.' "

"Odd topic to come up," I said.

"Well, I asked. In fact, I've been tracking you all evening. I want to hire you. Meg."

My neighborhood tap jockey came hustling in a way she never did for me. "Another Virgin Sunrise," Justin Ross told her and looked questioningly at me.

I shook my head. A pitch was coming; I didn't want to be behind the count if I didn't like it. Ross laid down a fifty as crisp as piecrust. "Give me half back, Meg. Mind if we move to a table, Mr. Rasmussen?"

I didn't mind at all. I was drinking his beer.

He chose the booth by the window, with an overhead light that displayed miniature Clydesdales hauling a beer wagon. We slid in across from each other. When Meg brought over the booze-free drink, Ross asked her if she'd be so kind as to call a taxi. To me he said he worked for someone well known who was coming to Lowell soon. Ross wanted me to handle security.

"You mean be a bodyguard?" I said.

"What we're looking at—" He broke off and nodded at the TV.

On screen, *Good Night Show* host Jerry Corbin was in his trademark pose, one hand on his heart, the other raised—"God's truth," it said—doing his monologue. "The other day I'm on Sunset," Corbin was saying, "and a big woman walking a Pekinese rushes up to me—I mean she was big."

"How big *was* she?" the audience roared on cue.

"*Big*. The size of a Fotomat booth. Had on these white stretch pants, and I mean s-t-r-e-t-c-h." Corbin spread his arms wide. "When she bent over to pick up her dog I thought I was at a twin drive-in." He paused for the laughs. "Anyway, she rushes up to me and screams, 'Jerry, I love you! I go to bed with you every night!' "

In chorus with Corbin, Justin Ross said, "No wonder I've been waking up with my pajamas pressed."

I looked at him. "Old joke?"

"I hope not. That was taped two days ago."

In Hollywood. Suddenly the tan and the cowboy getup made sense. And something else. "You're talking about Jerry Corbin?"

"Mr. Good Night America himself. You probably know that Jerry was born and grew up here in Lowell."

I did know, though not through any advertisement of the fact from Corbin. He was a hometown kid who had left and gone west thirty-odd years ago. He hadn't been back that I knew of, and Lowell never came up in his monologue. The city newspaper liked to drop his name from time to time.

Ross said, "The deal is, Jerry Corbin is coming to town. He'll be here next week."

Well, okay. Guy in late middle age, career on a downswing. Maybe he was having a roots experience.

"Remember the old *Gong Show?*" Ross asked. "From the sixties?"

"As in there's a *'new?'* "

He gave the quick smile, as genuine as his teeth. "You don't read *Variety*. Jerry's got a revival idea that has the network brass creaming their Calvins. He'll host; his company will produce. We'll go prime time, with plans to tape live in a bunch of cities. The pilot is here. Then on to Providence, Scranton, and Schenectady."

"Linchpin markets all," I said.

Ross's smile was tolerant. "Places where real folks live. I've been here setting it up. The city is eager to host him. Plus his alma mater is cooking up an honorary degree. The details have just been finalized, which is why there's been no fanfare yet—but once the word is out, it's going to be big."

"Big as a Fotomat booth?" I said.

No smile this time. He was used to heavyweights like Corbin. Actually, though, the news was interesting. Corbin hadn't burned up the Nielsens in a long time, and there were periodic rumors of replacements. Still, he was an institution, and he was from Lowell. The city hadn't got to honor a native show-biz kid since Bette Davis died, and she'd spent most of her life pretending the place didn't exist.

"The police will be involved, naturally," Ross said. "Crowd control, traffic details. But there's a reason I want you. And this is strictly confidential, regardless of whether you and I come to terms." Although we were the only patrons at this end of the room, Ross had lowered his voice. On the TV behind the bar, Jerry Corbin was flirting with a cotton-candy blonde I couldn't place. Off-camera, Corbin's second banana guffawed lasciviously.

"All right," I said.

Ross reached into his cowboy suit coat and took out a small plastic sandwich bag and handed it to me. The light from the beer lamp wasn't great, but it was enough to see there wasn't a sandwich inside. Peering through the plastic, I saw what looked like a greeting card, with a bright red outline of a heart on a sheet of beige industrial grade paper towel with serrated edges top and bottom. In the heart was a text formed of multicolored words cut from magazines and pasted down.

It was a finger-in-the-eye effect, like something you'd see on display if the Institute for Contemporary Art had a branch at Mass. Mental. The words said:

Back in the boneyard
you'll hear the Gong of Doom . . .

"That was sent to Jerry three days ago," Ross said. "It arrived at the studio. The woman who opens mail put it in Jerry's box without actually reading it; so by the time we thought to check the envelope, the trash had been picked up. She thinks it was postmarked Boston."

"Does the message mean something particular?"

He shook his head. "It's *crazy.*"

"Yet you took it pretty seriously."

"Jerry's no stranger to kook mail. He manages to piss off a fair number of people, but yeah. This seems elaborate. Somebody went to some effort."

Someone had. Despite the bright look, the note had a dark tone, a quality heightened by the fact that the cutting was ragged, as a lunatic negotiating a straight razor might create.

"You think 'Gong of Doom' refers to the new show?" I asked.

"It's a hell of a coincidence if it doesn't."

"Did you show this to the L.A. cops?"

"We didn't think it was much to go with." He stirred his mocktail, then lifted a shoulder. "The truth is, we're nervous about adverse."

As in publicity. It was one of those adjectives that some semiliterate flack had turned into a noun.

"The folks at network are edgy by nature," Ross went on. "If they got any hint that there might be a hassle, they'd ax the new show."

"I thought they were hot for it."

"TV's a fickle game. One idea—if they'd agree to do it anonymously—was to send that to the FBI for fingerprints or whatever."

"Ask them to solve the Cock Robin burn while they're at it."

He stared at me. "What?"

I said, "You can yank this paper off rolls in ten thousand public johns—no one keeps count. Plus, it's too absorbent for clean prints. You've got magazine cutouts here—big deal. And no direct threat. When I was a cop, I worked with the bureau a few times. They're good, but forget anonymous. You could paper the Beltway in their official forms."

Ross nodded slowly. "Point taken."

Corbin had become tabloid fodder again in the past year over another divorce—his third, I seemed to recall. And if memory served, his guest host was drawing bigger ratings than Corbin was, though you took your chances when you went on vacation as much as Corbin did. Ross said, "Do you know anything about television programming?"

The only TV I watched was right there in the Copper Kettle a few nights a week, when my apartment wallpaper was all reruns. "Nothing you'd want to hear," I said.

"If a show like this goes into production for one season—forget renewals, aftermarkets—one season, twenty-two episodes, in prime time? With a decent share and good ad accounts, you know what it stands to make?"

Okay, I'd be the straight man. "A lot of mazuma?"

"Try in the neighborhood of forty million bucks."

"That's a nice neighborhood to be in."

"We take this very seriously. But the police are out, for the time being, at least. And that's where you fit in. If that note is anything more than just a sick joke, you'd be responsible for making sure there isn't a punch line. And for trying to find the source."

"Maybe *I should* go after Cock Robin's killer," I said. "How long do I have to think about it?"

He glanced at his watch. "An hour from now I'm in Boston, climbing on the red-eye. You're right—it could be a tough assignment. But you've got a rep for being good and for not being an SOP guy. *I'd* like you, and I'd make it worth your time. But if you say no, I go elsewhere." He put the plastic bag back into his pocket. "Your move."

Decision time. I glanced at the fog swirling in the mild night outside. In a month, it could be snow. Come the holidays, you could bet Bobby Orr wouldn't be hanging around ice rinks. He'd be on a golf course, someplace warm and green, working on a tan like Justin Ross had. I gave Ross my winning smile. "What are private eyes for?"

"Good," he said.

I took a card from my wallet and handed it to him, pointing out that the pair of s's actually went with the second syllable, not the first. R-a-s-m-u-s-s-e-n. It was a printer's error, and I had a deck of five hundred, but the printer ran a shop as small as my own, so I had let him slide on it. He said he owed me. Ross made the correction with a gold fountain pen. "Want references?" I asked.

"I probably got the best one already." He nodded at Meg, who was standing over there behind the bar with her arms crossed, gazing up at Jerry Corbin. "She says you're the only person she knows who talks less and listens more than she does."

"Pshaw," I said.

Ross settled his briefcase on its side and thumbed the combination wheels. The hasps sprang open with a soft click. He took out a check ledger finished in the same skin as the briefcase and his boots, and opened it on the table. I had to ask.

"Ostrich," he said. "Ranch grown in Israel. These are quill pocks." The checks were painted with desert scenes in dusty pastels and drawn on a Jer-Cor Productions account at the Pacific National Bank of Santa Monica. He printed my name with the gold fountain pen.

"My fee is two-fifty a day, plus my out-of-pocket expenses. I like a two-day—"

The extra zero made me stop. He filled in the stub and tore the check out neatly, waving it once to dry the ink, then slid it over. The memo line said "petty cash account." The check was for five grand. I picked up the bottle of Molson and drained it to keep my hands from grabbing.

I asked to keep the note Jerry Corbin had received. When I had put it and the check in my inside jacket pocket, Ross said, "This has been easier than I'd expected. I'm sure everyone will be satisfied. I'm going to be in Los Angeles the next few days, but one of our people will be here starting Sunday night. She'll be your contact until the rest of us come. Her name's Chelsea Nash."

I wrote it down in my pocket notebook.

"If all goes according to plan, Jerry will arrive Tuesday evening, the twenty-seventh. We're booked for six nights at the Riverfront Plaza Hotel."

"This Ms. Nash," I said. "Who's she?"

"Jerry's personal assistant."

"I'd have guessed that was your title."

He flashed a bright smile—the first real one yet—and stood up. "I'm just a guy who gets things done." He glanced outside. "Time to saddle up."

I stood, too, and we shook hands again. "I look forward to working with you, Alex," he said. He called good-bye to Meg and went outside and got into the cab she had summoned.

I walked over to the bar and watched Jerry Corbin till the next commercial, all of ten seconds away, then put on my hat.

"First-class guy," Meg said.

"Top drawer." I did a fast body count of patrons, dragged out my wallet, and put down a moldy twenty. "A round for the house," I said.

As I walked down Middlesex Street toward Kearney Square, where my car was parked behind my office at Number 10, I paused on the bridge over the Pawtucket Canal. Above the thin fog and building tops, a horned autumn moon was pumping itself toward the full. The check in my pocket, with its mesas and saguaro cacti, felt good in there, warm, like an early Christmas bonus. If I'd had the gift of foresight, I might have been at the bank early next morn, cashing out my meager savings account and leaving for Cancún. At the very least, I'd have torn Jerry Corbin's check into confetti and cast it on the dark water.

2

I DIDN'T GET to the bank on Friday because I was at the beach all day. It wasn't vacation. I was at Hampton watching a thirty-eight-year-old city worker who had filed for disability retirement because of an injury she had gotten on the job. The insurance company smelled fraud. I had been at it three days; but so far, all I'd gotten was sunburn on my left arm.

Lowell had companies that went back nearly two centuries, like Locks and Canals—where Whistler's father had been chief engineer, long before son James had thought of painting his mom. And there were still city departments like Ashes and Waste, City Messenger, and Department of Maps: quaint sounding now, but they held on, like a lot of old habits. Like the work habit. Most people had it. They started early and stayed late and gave honest value for their pay. But there were always a few who looked for the golden goose. Part of me devoutly wished the insurance company was being paranoid, that the subject of my stakeout was just getting her due; and through no fault of her own she could live the beach life for a lot of years before *Modern Maturity* ever showed up in her mailbox. Maybe then the long hours I tended to put into the job when I was working would seem less of a sucker's game.

Around 3:00 P.M., as I was taking a break from a collection of André Dubus's stories and washing back fried onion rings with coffee, I saw the subject leave her rented cottage. She had forgone the walker this time in favor of an aluminum cane with four little legs on the bottom. Her handbag hung from her arm. I slipped the Kodak into my pocket, gave her a head start, and tagged along on foot.

We went up G Street onto Ocean Boulevard. Pedestrian traffic was light: retirees out for a jaunt, mostly, moms with strollers, beachniks combing for thrills. Sea gulls floated in the bright blue air. Just over the Massachusetts border in New Hampshire, Hampton Beach has always been a working family's vacation town, with a long strip of arcades, food joints, and surf shops facing the Atlantic, and behind it narrow lanes of rental shacks. But in the past decade, the honky-tonk charm had faded. The economy was part of it, and families stayed away. On sticky July days, the special police were on constant patrol of the crowds of teenagers who crammed the beach, and at night Ocean Boulevard was a strip for bikes and muscle cars, the air as rancid as the fat in the Fry-O-Laters at the clam joints. I had stopped to wait for a turning car, so I missed the actual contact, but I caught the next part.

A pair of young men on skateboards had approached the subject, one on either side. While one must have jostled the woman for distraction, the other grabbed her purse. They were weaving down the sidewalk now, coming my way. I saw the woman recover, shout something.

The kid with the purse—a lithe surfer blond—pitched it to his partner and peeled off down an alley. The second guy, a bodybuilder, kept stumping along in my direction. Not wanting to tip him that I was aware, I stopped and half-turned. As he came abreast of me, I used his momentum and hit him with a body check. He was top-heavy—all his meat in his chest and shoulders—and he flew from his skateboard. He banged off the shuttered front of an arcade. The purse popped open and spilled. Swearing, the guy got up fast. He rounded on me, fists clenched.

I smiled widely. "Ain't we got fun?"

He chewed that for a long second. In a gym, pushing metal around and posing for the women, he was probably a hot item—but a grinning middle-aged guy in a suit, talking from the 1920s, was beyond his realm, and a basic law of the jungle said: Don't mess with strange. He snatched his skateboard and bolted.

The woman arrived with miraculous speed. She squatted and started to gather her belongings. I sneaked two shots with the camera and stooped to help her. "You okay?" I said.

"If I'd a caught the little scumbags I'd a kicked their asses!" She grabbed her purse like it was full of disability checks; then, swearing under her breath, she trotted back toward where her cane lay shining in the autumn sun while I used the Kodak.

I drove back to Lowell, whistling all the way.

On Saturday morning I took a run along the Merrimack River. I looked at it as a life-insurance premium. I didn't have a payroll deduction, nor anyone anymore who I figured needed to benefit from my demise—though demise was far from my mind this glorious morning. Sumac blazed beside the paved path, and the river sparkled. Three miles is my routine, but I stretched it a little today, prodded maybe by the prospect of guarding Mr. Good Night America. Mine was a one-man show, and lately the only one buying my time was a Hartford giant. It was standard stuff—snooping at the Hall of Records, mostly—but I was grateful when it came . . . when it came.

The heyday of the big companies had passed. For years, Lowell had been Wang's World, complete with three corporate towers and bright blue flags spanking in the economic wind. It had meant a fair amount of security and investigative work. But time hurries on, and when Dr. Wang died, some piece of his dream died, too. Several hotshots had been in since, charged with keeping the company afloat. Downsizing, they called it, as if it were just a matter of a fat man having his pants altered; but after each new round, I would think of the U.S. general in Vietnam who had declared that the only way to save a hamlet had been to destroy it. It was a mental Möbius strip, with a logic you could examine all day but never find the seam.

Later, showered and suited, I drove downtown with the check and the cut-and-paste note that Justin Ross had given me. Outside my bank there was a group of people muttering about the CLOSED FOR BANK HOLIDAY sign on the door. I remembered why I called it the First Marginal. I went over to Kearney Square to the *Sun* building, where my friend Bob Whitaker is a news photographer. I told him I wanted several color copies of the note and asked what he would suggest. He scratched at his thinning Afro. "Well, I could use the copy stand, shoot it in Fujicolor, send it out for prints, get it back in a few days. Or"—he gestured toward a small gray machine—"we could use this. I'll make a negative, lock it into the scanner, set the computer for the right ASA and resolution. This'll read the negative and put it on the screen. It'll scan in the pixels, we can adjust tones, crop it, and get a final scan that'll look just like what you've got here. It's stored electronically, so we run it through a color printer, and you'll get what you want in an hour."

"If you say so," I said.

He burned off a photocopy for me, and while he went to the darkroom to make a negative, I went across the street and up to my third-floor office. I put the uncashed check in my safe, then gathered a stack of the magazines petrifying in my waiting room. Bypassing *Security Management Monthly* in favor of *Time, Newsweek,* and a few others, I took them in to my desk. After a half hour, I had confirmed that several of the words used in the cut-and-paste note sent to Jerry Corbin had come from national advertisements. Big deal. My coup, though, was identifying that Corbin's name, as used in the note, had come from the *Boston Herald.* A phone call to the librarian there revealed it had appeared on October 13 in the "Inside Track" column. This tended to confirm that the note had been sent from here and had been assembled within the past two weeks. Which narrowed the field dramatically: the *Herald*'s circulation was under a quarter-million.

"What is this, anyway?" Bob Whitaker asked me ten minutes later. He handed over the original note and prints he had made.

"Case I'm working on," I said.

The model of discretion, he let it go at that. I went down to the *Sun*'s morgue and dug the dirt on Corbin. I had been wrong about the divorces: there had been four. There was no current Mrs. Corbin. Ex number three, according to reports, was the hands-down winner in the alimony department. Also, Corbin's audience numbers *had* slipped over the past couple of years. I wasn't sure of the difference between a rating and a share, but then, who was?

The best source of general information was Corbin's obit, which the paper had ready to roll out when the occasion arose. I hoped it wouldn't be on my watch. From the piece I learned that Jeremiah James Corbin had been born in Lowell in 1937, had attended city schools, done a three-year hitch in the peacetime army, and had come back to attend the local state college. There he had been a member of the debate team, the dramatic society, and a brother in Kappa Tau fraternity. He had a B.A. in business, class of 1962. The college yearbook listed his heroes as J. D. Salinger, Sid Caesar, and jazz singers, and had named him most likely to do some "real gone thing" like swipe a DeSoto and head west. In fact, he had gone to Los Angeles (the article didn't say how he got there), had broken into television in the days of Jack Paar and Steve Allen, and had been working ever since. I phoned the university and asked for the alumni office, but they had bankers' hours, too.

3

AT 9:30 ON Monday morning, having deposited Jer-Cor Productions' $5,000 check in my NOW account, I appeared at the front desk of Lowell's best hotel. The Riverfront Plaza was a classy operation overlooking one of the locks on the city's old canal system. A young clerk with Valentino sideburns stepped over so smartly, I thought he might salute. His gold lapel tag identified him as Miguel.

"My name's Rasmussen," I said. "Is there a Ms. Nash registered here as a guest?"

He checked a list. "Chelsea Nash?"

"That's her."

He said she was registered but that she was out; however, she had left a packet for me. It was a large envelope designed to look like a TV screen. It held a press kit for Jerry Corbin's *New Gong Show.* It was first-rate fancy all the way through, including an 8 × 10 glossy of a smiling Corbin, his hand raised to God, swearing this was going to be *the* hot new show on network TV. I slid the pages back inside. "Did Ms. Nash say when she'd be back?"

"No, sir. But I hope it's soon." Miguel grinned. "You never seen her before, right?"

"Right," I said.

"She's cute. I seen her in the pool this morning, swimming

laps. She supposed to be famous or something? From California, I notice. And, I mean, who else gonna wear a name like Chelsea?"

"Nobody born within forty miles of Boston," I said.

Across town I found a parking spot on University Avenue. I drew in between a telephone-company van and a pale yellow Camaro splotched with primer. As I fed the meter, a university police car crawled by. I flagged it. A pair of campus cops was inside: one young, one old. With the wizardry of my ratiocinative skills, I figured if any place kept data on the old grads, it would be the alumni office. The cops directed me.

The campus was an oasis of calm: students strolling about in a kind of endgame of dewy innocence. Well, almost. A couple walked by in T-shirts that advised the world where it could stick what. In a quadrangle between dorms, football pep banners luffed in a breeze too mild to do much more than tease a few leaves out of the fluorescent maples.

I found Alumni Hall and hiked to the second floor. A woman with frothy white hair and clip-on earrings beamed when I explained what I wanted. "So it's true!" she said. "Jerry *is* coming to Lowell. You're the second person today who's asked about him."

Before I could say another word, a shrill noise seemed to come out of the air. I looked at the woman, and we both gazed around. Then the sound came again.

"Now what is *that?*" the woman asked, but I knew. Hackles had risen on my neck.

The sound had been a scream, and I identified its source as a heating register in the wall. Through the grid I could see a vent shaft. "Is there a basement?"

The woman gawked at me. "What? My goodness. Downstairs. Through that door. But you can't go down, it's . . . it's—"

I was moving. In the hallway other doors had opened, people standing in them, peering about uncertainly. I shoved through a set of fire doors to a stairwell and started down.

The stairway turned three times. I had heard no more screams, and the stillness filled me with both hope and dread as I reached the bottom. At the foot of the stairs there was a dim foyer. To the left was a janitor's closet; to the right a double door with opaque glass in the top panels and the words LADIES LOCKERS. I hesitated, listening, then eased open one of the doors and called in.

The room had a terrazzo floor and pale green tile walls that threw back my words. No other voice answered. I stepped in. Overhead ran the ductwork through which the scream had found its way upstairs. To the right were several closed toilet stalls and a shower room. Along the left wall stood a row of old wooden lockers. Partway down the row, half-crouched inside one locker, as if there hadn't been enough room for any other stance, was a woman. She had on a wine-colored nylon sweat-suit and running shoes. Her face was turned away, pressed into a corner of the locker, as though she were hiding from something. I glanced around to see what.

"Ma'am?" I said.

I went nearer. It took me a moment to realize she wasn't standing in the locker. She had a towel twisted around her throat, suspending her from a clothes hook.

I struggled to lift her off the hook, but there was little room to maneuver. With clumsy fingers, I fumbled at the knot in the towel. There was movement behind me, and I spun. A young woman with auburn hair and round tortoiseshell glasses came out of a toilet stall, bent over, wiping her mouth with her wrist.

I lifted out the hanging woman and laid her on the rubber floor mat. Her face was a dull gray, the color of ashes once a fire has died. I pulled off my jacket and spread it over her. I don't know if it was called for, but I needed to do something. I probed her throat for a pulse.

At that moment, the younger campus police officer I'd seen in the car charged in. He stopped. He looked at me, at the young woman standing bent over, the woman on the floor. He opened his mouth, then shut it. He was accustomed to panty raids, keys locked in cars. I thought he might follow the young woman's example and head for the porcelain. In that instant my fingers found a pulse. I said to the cop, "Get an ambulance."

He snapped the walkie-talkie from his belt and began barking into it. Bending close to the woman on the mat, I put my cheek near her face. I felt breath coming from her nostrils. It was faint, but there. My own breath came a little easier.

Beyond the opaque glass in the door, I could sense a crowd gathering. In a moment, fascination would overcome shock, and they would move in, gobbling air, trampling any evidence. I couldn't worry about that now.

The older campus officer from the car showed up. I told him what I knew. He instructed his partner to check out the rest of the locker room; then he squatted and looked at the woman. He moved slowly, lazily you might have thought; but it was a deliberateness I recognized, a habit of taking in details. I was pretty sure he'd been a city cop somewhere. Maybe deciding that all that could be done was being done, he looked at me and nodded. The young cop returned and said he'd found an outside door ajar. Together he and the older cop started rousting onlookers back out into the stairwell. I stayed with the woman. When the EMTs showed up I let them take over.

Back out in the hallway, I noticed the grandmotherly woman from the office upstairs. As if having heard that first scream together had forged a bond, she came over. She asked me did I know what had happened. I didn't. I said the woman inside was alive, though. While I was digging a card out of my wallet to give her, she whispered suddenly, "That's the one."

"I'm sorry?"

"The other person who was asking about Jerry Corbin." She nodded toward somebody standing at the edge of the crowd. It was the young auburn-haired woman who had been in the locker room being sick when I arrived—the one, it dawned on me now, whose screams had alerted us. I went over.

"Are you okay?" I asked.

She had on a pair of fashionably faded jeans and a green sweater and looked like a grad student. Behind the round tortoiseshell glasses, her green eyes were guarded, not meeting my own.

"Didn't you find her?" I said.

For an instant, she looked as if she might deny it. Then she nodded.

"What happened?" I asked.

"I don't know."

"How long were you there before I came?"

"I don't know. Two minutes."

"Was anyone else in there?"

She shook her head. She seemed eager to go. I asked her name.

"Jane Doe," she said abruptly. "Sally Citizen. I *found* the poor woman, I didn't put her there. This doesn't concern me."

"The police are going to think otherwise. They're going to want to talk. You can prepare yourself by trying to remember everything you saw."

Though I meant for them to calm her, my words only made her more nervous. I sensed she wasn't telling the truth—or at least not all of it—but before I could take my suspicion anywhere, the campus cops parted the crowd. The EMTs brought out the other woman on a wheeled stretcher. The onlookers, including the young auburn-haired woman, followed.

Remembering my jacket, I went back into the locker room. Someone had left it on a bench. As I was pulling it on, the door opened, and in walked Sergeant Ed St. Onge. He was followed by Gus Deemys, one of his detectives in the Major Crimes Unit of the Lowell PD.

Without a word of greeting, St. Onge motioned me to follow

and led the way around the bank of lockers to the other side. It was a changing area, made up of low wooden benches and a table where Babe Didrikson Zaharias might have taken her first massage. The smell of varnish mingled with the wintergreen sweetness of liniment. He pushed through an inner set of pebbled glass doors, and we stepped into a shower room. I guess he was assuming anyone who might have been using the facility when the commotion started wasn't now.

He checked each stall. I watched him. At the last stall, he reached in and turned the taps. Water hissed. Leaving the taps on, he rejoined me. He didn't look happy, but when in all the years I'd known him had he? His maroon blazer and gray slacks made him look like a middle-aged movie usher.

"Funny to find you here," he said in a voice that held not a trace of cheer.

"I happened to be on campus. I heard a scream."

"Happened to be on campus," he said. Steam began to rise behind him.

I shrugged. "I believe the key to a bright future is a sound education."

St. Onge and I had been friends for a lot of years. We and our wives had socialized when I'd been married. Thrown together originally by the uniform and badge, we were long past the former, and only he still swore allegiance to the latter. He still had a wife, too. Though neither of us had given it an epitaph, lately the friendship had frayed to threads of grudging mutual tolerance. He was right to be here, but I decided that mentioning I was working for Jerry Corbin was a needless complication. In terms of jurisdiction, what Corbin had retained me to do was of no concern to the cops. The weird note had been sent and received elsewhere, and it was Corbin's personal property. "I was upstairs," I said over the hissing shower. "Intending to do some research. I heard a scream."

"And you came down to help."

"Something wrong with it?"

"Good Samaritan Rasmussen."

"Can you remember that line for the reporters?"

"Cut the bullshit."

"What's this about?" I asked.

Steam was drifting from the shower stall. With his back to it, it appeared to be coming out of his body. "About you getting in the way—that's what."

"Who do you think told the campus PD to call an ambulance?"

"After you heard a scream and came down. Back up to that. We still haven't established what you were doing over here in the first place."

St. Onge wasn't a big man: five-ten, not heavy, but his was a toughness that made size secondary. His eyes looked like the snipped ends of steel rods, and his mustache was a flat gray line, like the horizon of your future. When it started to tip off kilter, trouble was headed your way. I'd seen him sweat confessions out of street hoods without ever raising his voice, though he wasn't above physical persuasion when he figured it was needed and wouldn't be reported. Mostly, however, his menace came in the form of his mind, which at times gave a sense of rolling several lengths ahead of your own—*my* own, at least. I didn't want trouble with St. Onge. Lowell is a small big-city. I needed the good graces of at least one cop with clout.

"An investigation brought me," I said.

His brow rose. "You've got a client?"

"It's not *that* unusual."

"Who?"

"This person isn't involved in whatever happened here."

The outer doors squeaked open and footsteps approached. Gus Deemys materialized. His silk suit glistened. He caught a glimpse of himself in a wall mirror and paused to look. The top portion of the glass was fogged. He bent his knees and touched his Windsor knot. Spotting us, he turned.

"What?" St. Onge said.

Deemys came over. I didn't exist for him. The blood was bad between Deemys and me; in fact, between me and most of the city heat. "We got the area taped off," Deemys said. " 'Attempted' is what it looks like. I got people checking for witnesses."

I said, "Did you speak with the young woman who found her?"

Deemys looked caught. St. Onge said, "The campus cop says *you* found her."

"Before me. She's the one who screamed. Reddish hair, nice-looking. Late twenties, maybe, jeans and glasses. Probably a grad student."

"Check it," St. Onge said. Deemys grunted and left.

St. Onge went into the shower stall and shut off the taps. "Okay, you did your civic duty," he said more equably. "The victim's on her way to Lowell General. And you've got a case that has nothing to do with any of this. So how about you make like the rest of the general public and disperse."

4

I GOT OUT of the steam bath with my pantcuffs still down around my shoes where they belonged. I looked for the young woman who had screamed, but the only people still around were St. Onge's crew hunting for clues. I fetched my car and headed downtown to the Riverfront Plaza Hotel. This time Chelsea Nash was in; but when Miguel called her room with my name, he listened a moment, then put his hand over the mouthpiece.

"She say she's busy and what you should do, you should make an appointment for tomorrow." He listened again and looked at me. "She say, how's ten A.M. in the morning?"

"Redundant, Miguel. Let me speak with her."

He handed me the phone.

"This is Rasmussen. You're Mr. Corbin's rep, are you not?" I said into the silence. "Shall I call him and say you aren't cooperating?"

"Are you always this surly?" a woman's voice shot back.

"I try, though occasionally I'm late."

The silence stretched a moment, then became a sigh. "Six-eleven. But don't plan to get comfortable. I've got a long to-do list, and you're pretty far down it."

Miguel grinned when I handed back the phone. "Smooth," he said.

I rode the elevator up to where the suites were. The corridor was thick-carpeted, hushed except for a room-service waiter clinking by, delivering late lunch or an early dinner. It was nearly 2:00, and I hadn't had either. I was in the wrong line of work.

The door marked 611 opened to the width of a safety bolt, and a vertical slice of face peered out at me. "It's you," said a voice trying to hide surprise.

As the bolt was unhooked and the door opened, I saw the face went with auburn hair and green eyes peering at me through tortoiseshell glasses. "And you're not really Jane Doe or Sally Citizen," I said.

Holding herself as if she were suddenly cold or nervous, the young woman from the campus stepped back to permit me to enter. "I don't have your contract, if that's what you're here for. It's being faxed today."

Room 611, I saw, was a large space with deep-pile carpet, white furniture, and vases that looked like amphoras, full of dried lotus pods and bare, twisted sticks that might have been wormwood. Short hallways spoked off to other rooms. I'd bet the pastel prints weren't screwed into the walls. I followed Chelsea Nash over to a sitting area formed by a couch and several big, soft chairs in nubby white fabric. Without sitting, she turned and folded her arms. "Okay, what did you want?"

Miguel's taste was as good as his hospitality. He'd go far. Minus the distractions of crisis, I saw how slender the woman was; fine-boned and medium height, but so well-proportioned that she looked tall. My age guess went up to early thirties. There was a slight outward cast to her right eye, barely noticeable except when she looked right at me, which was why I hadn't seen it before.

"Quite a coincidence," I said. It was either that or "Small world," and I'm nothing if not original.

"That was terrifying today," she said. "How is that woman?"

"Alive. Probably thanks to you. She's at Lowell General Hospital."

She nodded.

"What happened?"

"I only know what I told you."

I laid my hat on an end table and chose one of the white chairs. It billowed and sighed around me. When it stopped, I said, "Did you talk to Detective St. Onge?"

"The other one. Detective Deemys."

"How'd you happen to be there?"

"I was looking for a women's room. A student directed me."

"No bathrooms here?"

"You know, you can get annoying with these questions. The police interviewed me already. You're not a cop. You work for Mr. Corbin."

It didn't stop my curiosity, but she had a point. "So, let's talk about your boss and mine," I said.

She seemed willing, though I got the feeling she wished she'd been firmer on the phone. She didn't take a seat, which left me perched there on the puffy white chair, watching her. In my brown suit, I felt like a Fluffernutter.

"Mr. Corbin will arrive tomorrow evening," Chelsea Nash said. "I've spoken with the mayor and the city manager, and we're going to keep the arrival low-key. Rehearsals will start Wednesday morning. Friday evening Mr. Corbin will be honored by the city and receive an honorary degree, followed by a dinner. The new show will premiere live on Saturday night."

"Whew!" I said.

"It's a busy week. But Mr. Corbin is a pro. He and the crew have already been in rehearsal in Los Angeles for several weeks. We've sent out invitations to two hundred special guests. The rest will be first come, first served. Mr. Corbin wants the audience to be regular people." She was on her own turf now, enthusiastic. "That's Halloween night, which is perfect. It's going to be a costume party, with celebrity panelists. Seats will be a hundred dollars apiece, the money to go to local charities."

"And you want regular people?"

Daggers came from behind the schoolgirl glasses. In a gentler voice, I said, "You think the show will work?"

"Mr. Corbin has had some ups and downs this past year, but he's still got his finger on the American pulse. He's a great entertainer. Wait and see."

I was impressed with these people. Justin Ross called himself the person who got things done, but our Miss Nash wasn't letting the leaves go brown underfoot.

"Meanwhile, Mr. Rasmussen"—she moved a few steps toward the door—"I apologize for before. I was shaken by what happened. I hope that woman will be all right. But I wasn't joking about my to-do list. There are a thousand details to take care of, including your signed contract, which I'll have delivered to your office as soon as it arrives. So for now, if there's nothing else . . ."

I didn't rise. "Tell me about the note that Mr. Corbin received the other day."

That nicked a little cleft in her smooth forehead. "What about it?"

"Start with everything."

She went through it, making no apology for having tossed the envelope, though admitting that she wished she hadn't. In the staff meeting that followed receipt of the note, she said, she was the lone voice in favor of postponing the tour. Jerry Corbin had cracked jokes.

"Does Corbin have people out to get him?" I asked.

"*Mister* Corbin is loved by millions of people."

"A person needs only one good enemy."

She came nearer. "What do you intend to do?" Her eyes were wide and bright. The slight outward cast wasn't a flaw at all.

"I'd like to involve the police."

"I thought Jason was clear on that."

"Yeah. The note stays quiet until Mr. Corbin decides otherwise."

"That's his wish. He knows that if he goes to the police, it's certain to become news. That's why it's up to him to decide. He's been burned too many times by the media."

"There are worse ways to get burned."

It seemed to take something out of her. She sat on the edge of the couch. I said, "The point is, if I'm going to do what I've been hired to do, I have to have you people cooperating with me. Otherwise, you're wasting your money. Is there anything else I should know?"

"Like what?"

It wasn't much of an answer, but I accepted it for now. "Okay, if the cops are out, I suggest that you have Mr. Corbin get a bodyguard. Someone to be with him at all times. If I'm investigating this, I can't be in two places at once. You can arrange for someone, or I can—whichever you prefer."

She jotted a note. "I'll talk to Mr. Corbin."

"If you do it, get someone visible. The bigger and tougher the better."

"As big and tough as you?" she said.

"There isn't time for a nationwide search." I fought my way out of the chair and picked up my hat. At the door, I said, "One other thing—do you think what happened this morning has any connection to Mr. Corbin?"

"At the university? No. Why should it?"

There she went again: asking me to answer my own questions. I'd have to get a new approach. I hoped she was telling the truth, though; the thought of walking a thin edge with Ed St. Onge didn't cheer me.

Back at my office, I phoned Lowell General and asked about the condition of the woman who had been brought in—I still didn't know her name—but the person I spoke to didn't know what I was talking about. I let it go. I got out the press kit and spent some time going through that. By all accounts, Jerry Corbin was a world-class mensch. Show-business interviews invariably did that, imbuing their subjects with qualities that we lesser mortals seemed to have been born without. Even three of his four ex-wives said he was terrific, one big sweetie, though it's possible they had him confused with his alimony. No one had interviewed his mother. I noted that none of the press clippings was newer than a year old; most went back far longer. So what had been going on in Corbin's career in the past year? I had no answer and put the question on my to-ask list.

What I'd learned so far you could store under your thumbnail. I came back to the Corbin camp's insistence that the weird note not be reported to the police until Corbin chose to. Granting Chelsea Nash's concern that telling the cops would be tantamount to going public, she nevertheless had made it sound as though timing were important. Now, as I mulled it, I had the thought that what if, despite all protestations to the contrary, the note was a ploy? As publicity fodder, death threats to a star were as old as topless wannabes in the surf at Cannes—and with a new, unproven show about to open . . . I chided myself for my distrust.

I locked up and walked down three flights. As workouts go, it wasn't much—a little something for the quadriceps—but you took it where you could. Like work. Jerry Corbin's petty-cash check was in my bank account, drawing other money to itself like a dark suit drew lint. I brushed my lapels before hitting the street.

5

TUESDAY MORNING, OCTOBER 27, the sun still shone with unseasonal warmth. Fat pigeons cooed on the brownstone ledge outside the windows of my office. I sat at my desk with a second cup of coffee, reading the *Old Farmer's Almanac.* It had predicted the freezing rain we'd had earlier in the month and was calling for a bleak November, but for now Indian summer prevailed.

I wanted to call Ed St. Onge to ask about the police investigation of the attack at the university, but I couldn't figure a way. The *Sun* had carried an account and identified the victim as a Mrs. Florence Murphy, a university employee. Contrary to what St. Onge had told me, she had been taken to All Saints hospital, which was why I had drawn a blank at Lowell General. Now I wondered if it had been a deliberate misdirection on St. Onge's part. In another circumstance I might have just moseyed down to police headquarters, but I wasn't a welcome sight. As it did every time I thought about having lost my shield, the reason gnawed at me. Violation of Massachusetts General Laws chapter 268-A, section seventeen is what the court papers had called it. Taking a bribe is what it was. The thing was that had been the plan. A city councilman named Cavanaugh had been shaking down local developers who were looking to get a piece of the city's redevelopment action. People knew it, but there was no evidence to make a case. Working with my supervisor and a statie named Rydell, we set up a sting. Rydell put on a wire; I was to take the cash; when we'd got the deal on tape, we'd flash our brass. From the start, we should have smelled a rat. By the time the thing ended, Rydell had been shot in the face, the out-of-town gunman who'd shot him was dead, and I was standing there with a bag full of money. Funny thing: no recorder was found on Rydell. In time, he got his health back, but not his memory. There was a probable-cause hearing, with my supervisor and me crying setup. In the end there was no finding; but dirt sticks, and the department cut its losses. St. Onge's boss, Lieutenant Francis X. Droney—a/k/a the Ogre—headed the action, and I was history. To his credit, St. Onge had disobeyed the Ogre and had vouched for me when I applied to the state for an investigator's license.

Sounds came from my waiting room. Beyond the frosted glass, a figure appeared, followed by a knock.

"It's unlocked," I called.

The door opened to a woman wearing a long leather coat and carrying a black fabric attaché case. She stepped in briskly. "Hello, Mr. Rasmussen."

I rose. It took me a second to recognize Chelsea Nash. Her hair was pulled back in a French braid, and she had makeup on, but there was something else, too. "No glasses," I said.

"I'm wearing contacts. Now—"

"They mute the green," I said. "I like the green. Let me take your coat."

"Not necessary. I'll be brief. First—Mr. Corbin is scheduled to arrive this evening. Will you be available to come to the hotel at eight o'clock? Actually, that's Los Angeles time."

"Eleven P.M.," I said. "I know how to convert Celsius to Fahrenheit, too."

"If it isn't asking too much, he wants to see you." Her tone made it clear she did not share the wish.

"I'll be there."

"Fine. Second, we've hired a bodyguard. As per your suggestion. He'll be arriving with the group tonight. Do you have any questions?"

"Want to quiz me on metric to decimal?" I said.

"And third, I have your contract." But she didn't hand it over. She was a cool customer. Since arriving, she had been checking out the worn carpet, the gray metal desk and file cabinet, blinking as though what she saw were painful. Her eyes did look red. She nodded at the coat-closet door. "What's through there?"

"The secretarial pool and computer center, plus the lab where we test electronic snooping gear."

Her glance said some angry words. "Did Justin Ross come up here?"

"He hired me in a barroom. Would you care to inspect it?"

She frowned. "It's just that in Los Angeles the private agencies tend to be big gleaming affairs."

"In high-rise office towers. Sure, and you're buying Bauhaus rather than service, and Kookie parks the cars. They pass on the cost to the customer and pay criminal-justice grads from a junior college to do the footwork."

"Uh-oh," she said, "I think I hit a sore spot. I guess some private eyes are just unhappy, maladjusted men who use rudeness and crudity as armor to protect fragile egos."

"Damn right," I said. "You speak from experience?"

"Of course not."

"Did it bring results?"

Her eyes flashed, but I saw faint color rise in her cheeks. Her hands got busy opening the attaché case. "None of this has anything to do with why I'm here. Here's your contract." She dropped a sealed envelope on the desk. "I also brought . . . this."

It was a fax. The cover sheet was from Justin Ross and explained that the attached had arrived at Jer-Cor's California office that morning. I flipped to the second page and recognized what it was at once. The words said:

Your jokes grow whisper thin.
Gong time draws nigh.

I stared at them a moment, then looked at Chelsea Nash and gestured to a chair. She took it. I sat too.

"How'd you get this?"

"I've got a machine at the hotel."

"The police in on this one?"

"No. For reasons we've already discussed."

"So you're going to trust a malcontent with this?"

"I guess I have to. You've already been paid."

I read the note again. Even from the fax copy, it was clear that the format was the same as the note Justin Ross had given me: paper toweling with cut-out words. "Okay, Mr. Corbin's afraid the network brass will cancel his show if this leaks. That might've worked the first time, figure maybe it was a crank. Twice is twice."

"I spoke with Justin about it on the phone, and Mr. Corbin is firm."

"Have you got some pull with him?"

"I guess so, some."

"And what do you think?"

Chelsea exhaled softly and widened her eyes. The right eye had that slight outward cant to it, and they both looked redder than before. "That note's got a very freaky tone. It frightens me."

Freaky? All right, though I hadn't given up entirely on the idea that this was a publicity stunt. "Why don't you call Corbin right now? Let's make him change his mind."

"They've already left for the airport. Anyway, it's not that easy. Jer-Cor Productions is like a family—Justin, me, a few others—but Jerry calls the shots." She was blinking again, looking around. "Is there a ladies' room? If I don't take out these lenses . . ."

"In the hall. It's generic. But knock first, you never know who might've got in there."

She gave me a hot look and went out. I opened the envelope with my contract in it. The dollar amounts looked okay, and I stuck it in my desk drawer. Curious, I drew the attaché case over. There was a tag attached to the handle by a little leather thong. On it was Chelsea Nash's name, in care of Jer-Cor Productions in Burbank. I opened the case.

Inside was a stash of press kits for the new show. There were also a check ledger and a date book. Not looking for anything in particular, I paged through the ledger, skimming the stubs. The most recent checks had been written to a florist in Lowell and a talent agency in Boston. In a divided portion of the ledger was a petty-cash account. Several checks had been listed as "miscellaneous," including the one Ross had paid me as a retainer. That nettled me; I didn't like to think of my services as miscellany. One check had been written two days before to the estate of an Isabelle Martin for $11,300. It seemed like a lot for incidentals, though the five grand Ross had paid me hadn't bounced. I got a feeling they could tap the account all day, all week, all month if they had to and still be in petty cash.

Sooner than Chelsea Nash could have finished changing her eyes there was a rap on the door that rattled the glass. I slipped the ledger back into the case and went over and opened the door.

Ed St. Onge looked at me. Behind him, thumbing a moldy issue of *Sports Illustrated* in my waiting room, was Gus Deemys. He tossed it on the table. Deemys wore an Italian raincoat and natty gray felt hat with a darker satin band and a little yellow feather in it. St. Onge's garb didn't bear comment. In the same gesture, I waved them in and laid a manila envelope over the fax Chelsea Nash had brought.

St. Onge surveyed the office. "How's the private sector these days?" he asked.

"Well, you know. Between plugging ham-fisted goons and bedding leggy brunettes, there's barely enough time anymore to carry my receivables to the bank. It's why I quit charging fees."

"You better start again," said Deemys. "Who's your decorator, Robicheau Funeral Service?" He started to whinny, and I thought he'd elbow St. Onge.

"Who cloned Zeppo Marx, Ed?" I said.

Deemys's smile became a knife slash. "What do you, sit around here all day thinking them up? Get plenty of time for it, don't you? And maybe you're gonna have a lot more pretty soon."

"All right, shut up," St. Onge said, still looking at me.

"What's going on?" I said.

"I ask questions, you give answers. What was this doing over at the university?" He held one of my cards, probably the one I'd given the grandmother in alumni affairs.

"So I can't afford a TV spot," I said. "Is honest poverty a crime?"

"You're doing it again. So let's get to it. You were over there bracing people about yesterday's assault. That's interfering in a police investigation. And that's after I told you to keep away, which also makes it refusing a police order." He held a thumb and forefinger an inch apart. "You're skating this close to the hole in the ice that swallows up smart-asses."

"I told you," I said.

"This close."

Just then the door opened and Chelsea Nash came back in. With her round-framed glasses on and her face scrubbed, she was back in school. She was startled to see the others there.

Deemys appeared equally surprised, but recovered faster. He touched the knot of his tie. "Morning, ma'am."

St. Onge glanced at me then stepped aside and added greetings.

Chelsea pushed up her glasses and flushed. "Hello."

"This is Detective Deemys. I'm Sergeant St. Onge," Ed reminded her.

"Yes . . . I remember." She glanced darkly at me, and I knew what she was thinking.

"Why don't we all sit down," St. Onge said. He made it sound like a suggestion, but no one was fooled. No one sat, either. Deemys stood by the door, his hands in his coat pockets; I stayed beside my desk. "You know, ma'am," St. Onge went on, "this makes each of our days a little easier. I was going to come see you later."

"Oh?" Chelsea was off balance. I was too. Why hadn't she gotten herself locked in the bathroom? "What about?" she asked.

"Coincidence. But this seems to be a time of coincidence." He glanced at Deemys. "The moon full or something?"

"Not till Halloween," I said helpfully, patting the almanac.

"You mentioned that you're staying at the Riverfront, visiting from California," said St. Onge.

"That's right." Chelsea seemed uncertain of what role she was expected to play. I couldn't help because I didn't know either.

"Consider this one a moment. A woman who works in the university alumni office claims two people came in there separately yesterday morning asking about Mr. Jerry Corbin, who, as I don't think either of you needed to read last night's newspaper to know, happens to be coming to town tonight. From L. A." St. Onge's tone had taken on an exaggerated patience. He settled on a windowsill, his gaze on Chelsea Nash. "You didn't mention, ma'am, that you work for Jerry Corbin."

"No," she murmured.

"Why not? He's a celebrity."

"I guess I didn't think it was necessary. When I talked with you, I was still finishing contract arrangements. I didn't want to complicate that with publicity. Besides, none of that has any bearing on what happened to that poor woman yesterday."

"You may be right. What about you?" St. Onge said to me. "I suppose when I ask who you're working for, you're going to play it dumb."

"Uh-uh. Smart," I said. "I want to stay in business. I want to keep getting clients."

"You won't need 'em without a license," Deemys said. "I say we bust this coin-op cop, Ed."

"That your answer?" St. Onge asked me.

I squeezed around behind Chelsea Nash and went over and opened my office door. "Since we're on the subject of coincidence," I said, "it just came to me, Ed, that, scrambled, your name is an anagram for 'gone.' "

"What're you going to do if we don't? Call nine-one-one?"

"You're better when you play straight man to the wits you work with," I said. "There's nothing I can say you don't already know; the rest I'm just not going to. I was square with you yesterday. If you'd thought harder, you'd have figured out I left my card *before* any of that action happened. You're the one who got sneaky, telling me the Murphy woman had gone to Lowell General. Now you come on with tough. I didn't like the roust when I was a cop, I like it less now."

Deemys shoved his fists deep in his pockets and spread his raincoat open. "Too bad, Coin-op." I guess the gesture was supposed to be menace. He just looked like an overdressed flasher. With a sigh, St. Onge pushed off the windowsill and motioned Deemys to lead the way out. At the door, St. Onge looked at me. He didn't say a word. Didn't have to. I got the message.

So much for fence-mending. When they had closed both doors and clumped down the hall to the elevator, I sat on the edge of my desk and said to Chelsea Nash, "I've got a problem."

"With them?"

"And you."

"What? I don't know what you're talking about. I'm leaving."

I gripped her attaché case.

"Give me that," she said.

"Lady, you may think this is live television, for your entertainment, but I can lose my license. Cops don't like being fooled with. St. Onge takes it especially badly. What do you know that you're keeping from him?"

"Nothing. I resent—"

"So do I! We're supposed to be on the same side. What's Florence Murphy got to do with this?"

She flinched at my raised voice. "I have no idea."

"And you just happened to be at the university yesterday."

"Yes. Now give me my belongings."

"Who's Isabelle Martin?" I said.

Her eyes got angry—then scared. I let go of the attaché case. "I was doing the same thing you were doing there," Chelsea said. "I was at the alumni office trying to get information on Jerry Corbin. I went there to find out about . . . his past."

I took my chair for that one. "What could you learn there that you don't already know?"

She shook her head, looking pained. "Nothing," she said quietly. "And that's the truth. Now may I go?"

6

The Kappa Tau house was a big gray clapboard affair on Mount Hope Street, with red shutters and a ramshackle porch, and the Greek letters painted over the entrance. I seemed to recall it as being the frat where a student had tried to do himself in a few semesters back by drinking a whole bottle of Maalox. A fuzzy toy spider hung on the door. I pressed the bell. In a paved side yard, several young men were tossing a Frisbee, playing keep-away from a game mongrel. The dog's tongue lolled like a ribbon of pink rubber. One of the young men yelled, "Doorbell don't work. You gotta knock hard." I waved and did so.

Across the street, a guy with a blower was cleaning his lawn, sending leaves cartwheeling down the sidewalk to become somebody else's problem. I watched. If machines mirrored the people who made them, the leaf blower was the perfect twentieth-century American device. Most of the lawns had bright-colored campaign signs pegged in them, promoting next month's city elections. I didn't see the same candidate's name twice. The door opened. A young man with a Pats T-shirt and a flushed face stood there, zipping his fly. Like the guys in the yard, he was on the large side. He looked at me as if he expected me to give a password.

"Hope I'm not interrupting," I said. "I'm looking for Vito." I had phoned ahead and been given the name.

"Oh, you the guy about Jerry Corbin?"

"That's me."

He glanced past my shoulder, probably to see if I had a photographer with me to put him in *Playgirl:* "The Hunks of Kappa Tau." Disappointed, he motioned me in.

The house had once been elegant, if you went by the fifteen-foot ceilings, leaded-glass windows, and classical columns; but alas, no more. The oak floor fairly cried for varnish, and there were fraternity letters spray-painted on the walls, as if someone held practice runs before going out and defacing rocks along Route 3. The decor was Greek, all right: spartan. Beer kegs for end tables, sprung easy chairs and shelves of *Cliff's Notes.* I quit wondering where the sign for Middlesex Street had gone.

A green lava lamp blurped on a packing crate in one dim corner. Near it, on a rumpled couch, pretending to study a trigonometry book, sat a rumpled brunette.

"Midterms," the guy in the T-shirt said.

"No pain," I said, "no brain."

"I'll get Vito." He disappeared farther into the house. I peered into a side room and saw three guys sitting at a round table, drinking from quart bottles of beer and jotting things on paper. "Cramming for their mixology exam?" I asked the brunette.

"Friday night's Halloween," she said. "They're the party planning committee."

I nodded. Seemed like an easy gig, figuring out how many cases per person you'd need. The brunette said, "You're not pledging Tau are you? Being as I never seen you."

"No."

"I thought you seemed kind of old. No offense, hey."

I let it alone.

My host reappeared and told me right this way. We went through other ill-furnished rooms to the foot of a staircase. "Yo, Vito!" he called up. "I'm sending him up." And to me: "Top floor."

Like most of the house, the stairway held little trace of bygone glory: Scarlet O'Hara would never sashay down it on Rhett Butler's arm. It groaned beneath worn rubber treads, and the gap-toothed banister wobbled. At the top, a small fellow with wire-rim glasses was waiting. He had on chinos and a white polo shirt with the collar up and wore the look of the perpetual club historian. Ten years ago, he probably had overseen the tattered stash of skin mags in his neighborhood tree hut. We greeted each other and shook hands.

"Yeah, Jerry Corbin was a brother," Vito said, leading me back into the upper floor. "Which, like, I knew, 'cause someone mentioned it when we were pledging, but it's nothing anyone made a big deal of. Not like Leo St. Hillaire making All-Pro with the Broncos. He was a brother, Leo. Anyway, I looked up Jerry Corbin after you called."

"What did you learn?"

"Not much. The house files are kind of in a shambles." He said it with an apologetic frown, as though this were an unexpected oversight here. "His name is on the rolls back in the early sixties. He was on the Greek Week float and the homecoming committees. He played frat football. For all practical purposes, that'd be the story on Big J."

"Big J?"

Vito treated me to a sly look like he'd made a find that would seed masters' theses for years to come. "What he was called. Come up here a minute"—he opened a door—"I want you to see something."

The doorway opened on a flight of steps, boards nailed directly onto the stringer, no risers. I followed Vito, and we emerged in a hot attic, lit only by a dusty skylight. Wasps buzzed, and the trapped air had the tang of insulation dust. I had to stoop until we reached the pitched height at the center. Visible in the gloom, as my eyes adjusted, were a moth-eaten moose head and the chassis of what once had been a chariot float. Festoons of old crepe paper hung from it. Vito pointed up. "There," he said.

On a thick rafter, something was written in what appeared to be charcoal. I had to squint to read it. *Big J planked Betty Crown 4/25/62.* There were other markings on the rafter, though none of the names was Corbin's.

"This used to be like a house totem pole," Vito said with a kind of vicarious pride. The most recent date I saw was 1982. The verbs changed too. It was a pop-cultural history of sexual slang.

"Any idea who Betty Crown was?" I asked.

"Some hot party girl, I figure, which is why her name's here. There've been a lot of them over the years." Vito stood on tiptoe to run his fingers down the splintery wood, as if it might bring him luck.

"If these walls could talk," I said.

Sweating, we picked our way back across the planks. "So that's the complete file on Big J?" I said when we had descended the steps.

"Seems like he was a regular guy. Lots of babes. Pulled okay grades."

"And now he's Mr. Good Night America."

Vito nodded. "I was thinking like maybe I should do up an article for the school paper. Get some press for the house." For an instant his eyes may have glowed with the light of reflected glory, a small man in a house of large men. Then it faded. "But nah, if I don't, like, ace a couple midterms, *I'm* history."

I took out my wallet and extracted one of my cards and two twenty-dollar bills. His eyes clamped on the bills. I aligned them face to back. "Would a monetary inducement interest you?" I said.

"To dig some more?"

"Sure. And write your piece if you want to."

He scratched his nose. "Well . . . cool."

I tore the bills in half. I handed him two halves, along with the card. "If you get me anything else about Big J, I'll give you these." I put my halves into my shirt pocket.

He tried matching his, but came up only with a mutant Andrew Jackson. "How long've I got?"

"Couple days. After that, we can both pin them on the wall and write *'tempus fugit'* underneath."

Vito walked me downstairs. The planning committee was still in closed session, probably trying to figure out whether to decorate in orange and black or vice versa. Outside, the neighbor's lawn was clear of leaves, and he and his blower were gone. The guys with the Frisbee were gone, too. I looked around for the young dog. Ditto.

7

AT 10:55 THAT evening, I rode the elevator to the top floor of the Riverfront Plaza Hotel. I smoothed my hair and cinched up my tie. It wasn't every night I got to meet a legend. I heard the festivities before I was halfway down the corridor: music and talk and the plink of glasses. I knocked on the door where the sounds were loudest. As I waited, I stepped over to a window and looked out. A three-quarter moon glowed in the autumn sky, brushing the buildings with gold. There were leaves still on the trees, and street lamps threw bright circles among them. Beyond, the river was scaled with moonlight. Like a lot of cities, Lowell looked better the higher up you went. From a blimp it could win beauty prizes.

I was about to knock again when the door opened. The guy who opened it stood medium height, but that was the only thing medium about him. His shoulders filled the doorway. He was a hulk of tanned, gym-trained muscle, with veins snaking over his biceps. He was in a faux leopard-skin tank top and baggy white crepe slacks, held aloft with purple suspenders. His golden hair was sculpted in a pompadour that surfed over his broad forehead and curled just off his earlobes, in one of which a diamond stud winked like a stage light. He wore espadrilles the same pale blue as the long-lashed eyes he had clamped on me. For a moment I wondered if I was at the right room, or in the right hotel, or even in the right city. Then I spotted Justin Ross inside, talking to people. I told the guy at the door who I was.

His manner changed. "Hey, all right! Good to see you."

When he finished crushing my hand, I squeezed past him into the alcove while he did a quick scan of the corridor and shut the door. "Are you packing, Mr. R.?" he asked earnestly.

"Not I."

"Gonna have to frisk you anyway. Sorry."

Why not? I spread my arms. "No tickling," I said.

He did it efficiently, moving right down to my shoes. "Okey-doke." He rose. *"Entrez vous."*

"Thanks," I said, and was tempted to whisper that I'd helped get him his job, but that might have made him self-conscious.

The suite was even grander than the one Chelsea Nash occupied. There was the big main room with a balcony facing the canal, the French doors of which were open now, a soft breeze moving through them, stirring chintz drapes. A hallway led to other rooms. I guessed the crowd at twenty, an assortment of show-biz types by the looks of them. The doorman stood out by just a little. Nancye Tuttle, who writes entertainment news for the *Sun* was there, in her element. To one side, on a long table, was a spread of food and champagne. I went over and took a plate for something to do. The centerpiece was a cornucopia fashioned of braided bread, spilling out a medley of fresh vegetables and fruits. The guests had ignored them; I did, too. I used toothpicks to spear a few cocktail franks.

"Alex, good. I'm glad you're here."

Justin Ross had detached himself from the guests. We shook hands. He had on a cowboy suit in pale gray denim, with a blue bandanna knotted at the neck, and his ostrich-hide boots.

"Where'd you find Austin Tayshus?" I asked.

"Who?"

I pointed a toothpick at the doorman.

"He's something, isn't he? We got him through an agency in Los Angeles."

"He works for a *detective* agency?"

"A talent agency. His name is Phil Gripaldi. He does stunt work. We could have had a Mr. T look-alike."

"But why draw attention?" I said.

"Is he a problem?"

"I wish it were a black belt for karate holding up his pants, instead of lavender braces. Has he got any training—besides Method acting, I mean?"

"He's big."

I frowned. "Maybe the getup will keep the focus away from Mr. Corbin. It's working so far. Where is he?"

"Jerry? We'll get to that." Ross lowered his voice. "Have you learned anything yet?"

I said I hadn't. I wanted to ask him the same question—I assumed I hadn't been called up here just to party, and nobody was breaking their neck to introduce me around or get me a drink—but Ross appeared eager to get to something else. I trailed him into a small adjacent room, where a short roly-poly fellow with a mustache and a rumpled suit sat munching a sandwich as he poked a calculator. There was also a fax machine, a photocopier, and several telephones. Ross introduced the man as Jer-Cor's accountant, Morrie Vining. Give him a floppy white hat, and he was the little guy on the take-out pizza box. He eyed me a moment, then was back at it, crunching long strings of figures that seemed to come out of his head as continuously as the tongue of paper tape curling from his machine. As Ross led me away, I asked, "Was that a calculating look he gave me?"

"If anyone in the entourage spent a quarter on a pay toilet today, Morrie's got it figured in the P and L. He keeps tight charts."

"I'll bet they're pie charts."

Ross knocked on a door, opened it and peered in, then nodded me through behind him. Five people were standing around a large TV set up on a table along with a VCR. They were drinking champagne and watching something on the screen, which faced away from me. The lone woman was Chelsea Nash. She was wearing black pants and a hot-pink blazer, and in heels was as tall as all but one man in the group. They glanced over. It was the tallest man—the oldest—who said gruffly, "What?"

Ross said, "Uh, gentlemen, can we have a few minutes?"

The three younger men excused themselves, measuring me with looks as they filed past. Ross shut the door behind them and led me over. Chelsea Nash snapped off the TV and VCR. Ross said, "Jerry, I'd like you to meet Alex Rasmussen. Alex, say hi to Jerry Corbin."

Cathode-ray magic had fooled me again. On-screen, Jerry Corbin looked rangy and fit, projecting a healthy, happy image; a man who, despite life's vicissitudes, never lacked good humor. Standing three feet from me now, as we shook hands, sans makeup and trick lighting, he had a pallor that, for a Southern Californian, meant work. He wasn't smiling, either. On the tube, the large-boned frame was robust; but there was a sedentary softness to him in person, accentuated by his height. And the suit—from the collection that bore his name, I guessed—was rumpled. Still, in spite of the details, he was a presence. He radiated something that was bigger than he. I squared my own shoulders. "Hello," I said.

"Alex, welcome aboard." We shook hands. Corbin's grip was firm, his gaze overbright. "You know Chelsea."

"Yes," I said. I glanced her way but she wasn't looking.

"What're you drinking?"

"Am I working?"

"Light duty. We're getting acquainted. Champagne?"

"Beer, if you've got it."

"Chelsea, honey, a beer for the man—and find the key for that damn machine there and get me a Dewar's, would you?"

He motioned Justin Ross and me over to a sitting area. With horror I saw the chairs were the big marshmallow jobs. The expressions on Corbin's and Ross's face told me it was a first for them. We made small talk a moment, and by the time we stopped sinking I had a Mill City ale in my hand. Chelsea took two nip bottles from the mini-bar, got ice and a rocks glass and fixed a practiced double, which she handed to Corbin. Smart woman that she was, she drew up a wooden chair to sit in. When Corbin had taken a healthy knock of Scotch, he said, "Got that note?"

Ross produced it and handed it to me. Same format as the other two: cutout words pasted onto industrial-grade paper toweling. This time they were inside a pumpkin outlined in orange crayon. The words said: *W. F.'s Stockholm address. You won't even hear it.*

Ross said, "It came last night."

Corbin said, "Shit, I don't mind being hassled—I get paid enough, I expect it—but at least the sonofabitch could make *sense.*"

"You have the envelope?" I leaned forward to get some movement in the chair.

Ross passed it over. It was addressed to Corbin here at the hotel, marked HOLD FOR ADDRESSEE. Inked on the corner, overlapping the stamp, was a clear cancellation mark: Cambridge, MA, with an 02141 zip code and yesterday's date.

"Know anyone in Cambridge?" I asked.

The three of them exchanged a glance. Corbin said, "Not really."

"Sweden?"

"No."

"Who or what's W. F.?"

Shrugs. I looked at the note again and had an image of someone sitting at a kitchen table in a pool of faint light, cutting words, pasting the backs and sticking them to the paper, then using a fat orange crayon. The someone was just a shadowy figure.

Corbin said, "What do you think?"

"Does anything in any of the notes make sense? How about 'Boneyard'?"

"Nothing."

I glanced at Chelsea, but she kept her green eyes elsewhere. Since I'd entered, she had been ignoring me studiously. I said, "I think you should call the cops."

Corbin didn't jump on me. In fact, he didn't speak at all. He glanced at his watch. It was Justin Ross who, fingering the bandanna around his neck, said, "Mr. Rasmussen, do you know anything about the mass media?"

Just call me Marshmallow McLuhan, I thought. I said, "Enough to understand your wish to avoid bad publicity right now."

"Damn right," Ross said. "So if I were to go to the local police with the notes, this moment, what do you think they'd say?"

"You? In person? Probably 'yippee yi yo ky yay,' " I said. "But you're right. There's no guarantee they would or could keep it quiet."

Corbin grinned. "Yeah, and the Godfather of Insomniacs could go straight to the ash can without getting a chance to be King Gong. So for now, and until further notice, the existence of the notes remains known only to this group. How swear ye?" He raised his glass and looked at Ross, then at Chelsea, and finally at me, and we all gave assent. "Good. And now—to success, all around."

Chelsea fixed another course of drinks; only one nip in Jerry Corbin's glass this time. She and Ross stayed with fizzy water.

Corbin said, "To old friends. Life, liberty, and the pursuit of whatchamacallit."

He drank and laughed, and we all did. The mood grew convivial. He had that gift of making people feel happy, and although I sensed that surface good cheer and booze were part of it, I liked the man. It was clear the others did also. When we'd finished one more round, I got out of the chair. If I didn't then, I'd have to sleep in it. I tugged my suit coat straight. "Will you need me to stay at the hotel while you're in town?" I asked.

Corbin waved his arm. "It's early yet. Have another drink."

"I'll take a rain check, Mr. Corbin. It may be early Pacific time, but I've been here all day."

Justin Ross rose, too. Corbin struggled a moment with his chair, then gave up and stayed put. Ross said, "I think we're okay for tonight. We can hash out arrangements tomorrow, and if it makes sense, you could stay here."

"Or you could all come over to my place," I said.

Corbin got his hands on the remote tuner and activated the TV set. The late weather was on. "Let's get on with the show," he said in a slightly thick voice. "The monologue, at least. The guests are dog meat, as usual, but the monologue'll get 'em."

Justin Ross ushered me out. In the main room of the suite, the crowd had thinned. Nancye Tuttle had her notepad and was talking to Phil Gripaldi, he of the purple suspenders. She knew a story when she saw one. I got my hat. I tried to catch Chelsea's eye, but she was speaking to Morrie, the accountant. As I headed down the plush corridor, I could hear Ross in full voice, rallying the troops, marching them into the master bedroom to catch *The Good Night Show.* One big happy family.

Passing through the hotel lobby I heard a jumpy piano rendition of "Do You Know the Way to San Jose?" On an easel by the lounge door was a placard with a glossy publicity photo. "LIMITED ENGAGEMENT," the copy said, "THE INIMITABLE STYLINGS

OF MARTIN AT THE BALDWIN." I was going past when a voice I knew said, "Slumming?"

Ed St. Onge was leaning against a pillar, his hands in his pockets. He had on one of his vintage suits: pinch waist and flared cuffs. Give him a ruffled shirt, and he could have been a skip from Carnaby Street, on the lam the past twenty-five years. His cheeks were shadowed to the same dark hue as his mustache, and there were bags under his eyes.

"I suppose you're being a good doctor making late rounds," I said.

"I'm done for the day. Been working on that assault over at the university. There's a puzzler." He said this without changing anything in his expression, including the lock his eyes had on mine.

"And you probably figured you'd lay it out for me and get an easy solve," I said.

He nodded toward the lounge. "One for the road?"

I wanted to pass, but his being there by chance at that hour was about as likely as my being mistaken for Christopher Reeve.

The lounge light was softer, though "magical" would have been going too far. Most of the patrons were business overnighters, no more stoned than Jerry Corbin. A guy with black hair, who might have been the older brother of the guy in the glossy, was seated in a spotlight at a baby grand with a big snifter on top for tips. Seeing us come in, he raised his eyebrows and smiled. The song became "I Say a Little Prayer for You." St. Onge and I sat at the bar. He ordered V.O. and a Bud. I stayed with Mill City and began nibbling from a bowl of spicy cocktail mix.

Puffing smoke, St. Onge said, "Figure, the Murphy woman wasn't carrying her purse, and she's not the type you want to tackle—she's an exercise nut. Everybody thinks the world of her. So 'why?' is the question."

"You been able to ask her?" I said.

"The doctors want to give her another day or two before we talk."

"Well, I'm glad she's going to be okay," I said. I offered him the bowl of spicy peanuts and pretzels.

He scowled. "Stuff gives me more gas than Exxon."

I snatched the bowl away. He drank beer, then set the glass down and hit the V.O. I told him it was supposed to go in the other direction.

"Hard to see in this light," he said. "Besides, I'm a little giddy tonight. Being in the vicinity of stars does that to me."

I didn't bite.

"This isn't your kind of joint," he said. "Not at four bucks a toss."

"I like to play fast and loose with the cocktail mix."

"Your client is Jerry Corbin. You been upstairs tucking him in?"

"Jerry Corbin? From *The Good Night Show?*"

"Knock off the crap, Rasmussen. The TV news people were crawling on him at the airport tonight. He's here. The desk confirmed it. What's he got you doing, peeping on one of his exes to try to ease an alimony sting?"

"*The* Jerry Corbin?" I repeated.

He waited. He was good at waiting. I listened to the music a moment. "I'll Never Fall in Love Again." Martin at the Baldwin was good, too; he actually remembered enough Burt Bacharach tunes to put together a medley, and it sounded fine. "Okay, Corbin hired me," I said. "But don't be coy, Ed. What you're really asking is if there's a connection with the attack on the woman at the university."

He crushed out his cigarette. "And?"

"You think I'd hold out on you if it was important that you know?"

He ran that one for a moment, then made a movement with

the side of his mouth that I think meant acceptance. The set ended and Martin walked by, glancing a question my way as he passed.

"Prospective client?" St. Onge said.

"Shamus to the stars."

He finished his beer and set the mug down. I didn't ask him if he wanted another. He said, "Okay, we'll assume it's coincidence. If Corbin is making news, I want it all to be good. I happen to like the guy. He's my favorite comedian, along with Red Skelton and Jerry Lewis. But I don't want cute going on in my city. You follow me?"

"Yeah," I said. "But you left out Benny Hill."

After St. Onge was gone, I ordered a black coffee and drank it slowly. Back at the Baldwin, Martin slipped into a new medley: city songs this time. Chicago, New York, San Francisco. I didn't strain my ear listening for Lowell. On my way out, I stuffed a buck into the snifter.

8

WHEN I HAD fetched my car from the hotel garage, I didn't go home. Never mind that it was long past midnight and I'd been working all day. St. Onge had put a fishhook in my brain.

Across the city, I parked on University Avenue and started to walk. The campus was still, hushed in the autumn fog, which swirled around the sodium lamps and made a sighing carpet of the leaves underfoot. Impelled by a new curiosity, I moved along branching paths. I saw no students, not even sober ones. At last, I spotted the building I wanted. It was dark and locked, but I had expected that. What I didn't expect, as I made my way around the side, was to see someone coming out of the rear door by the old locker room where someone had attacked Florence Murphy yesterday morning. The person was wearing a coat with a drawn-up hood, pointed on top like a cowl.

"Excuse me," I called.

I might as well have said, "Give me your wallet." The person vaulted over a railing and started to run. Debating for just a moment, I went after him.

The path wove among clumps of bushes. In the fitful lamplight, I could see the person running ahead, the pointed hood giving him an alien look. He never glanced back. Coffee, beer and party mix sloshed in my stomach. Fallen leaves made my footing uncertain, but I didn't push it. I'd been doing fifteen to twenty miles a week for years; unless he did more, over the long distance he was mine.

When he reached University Avenue, he cut around a parked van. A car alarm went off, startling him. He darted across the road. The alarm was one of those sonic smorgasbords. As I reached the van, the siren went to whistles.

I got across the road and reentered the darkened campus. Through the trees I saw the person disappear around the side of a building. The sloping ground brought me into a grove of pines, angling down alongside Pawtucket Boulevard. Across that was the river. In the grove, where only random shafts of light got through, I couldn't make out the contour of the ground. Our footsteps shushed through pine needles. I wondered what I'd do when I caught him. Far behind, the car alarm provided a fading sound track: banshee wails, wolf howls, falling bombs.

The ground dropped abruptly, and my pelvis jarred against my diaphragm and lungs with a *whoof.* I just managed to keep my balance. I struggled on for a few more strides, but I had to stop. When I emerged from the trees, walking now, my quarry was gone.

Disappointed, I stood listening for retreating footsteps. Who was he? Why had he been there? I thought about going back to the alumni building, but I had grown aware of another sound, one that was part of the night around me. It was a low, mechanical humming. I moved toward it, going around big clumps of bushes. Farther on, the trees ended. I saw a vapor lamp, aswirl in the mist like an occluded eye. I skied halfway down an embankment overgrown with goldenrod and sumac. At the bottom I came to a squat building made of yellow brick, which I realized was the source of the humming sound. The campus steam plant.

I peered through a large window covered with wire mesh. Just enough light fed through from outside to reveal ductwork and a huge old boiler. There was an outside stairwell, with a metal-sheathed door at the bottom. I went down and pulled the handle, feeling my heart catch as the door grated open over dead leaves.

The room was dominated by the boiler, a massive asbestos-covered monster, with ducts running off from it like tentacles. Beyond it I could just make out a dark corridor. Somewhere faint music was playing. I edged ahead, one hand extended to catch spiderwebs and the occasional low-hanging pipe. As I rounded the boiler, a weak light came on. I whirled to see a figure lurch toward me.

"What's goin' on?" he cried, swinging something above his head.

I got my hands up. *"Whoa!"*

He edged into the light of a naked bulb, and I saw he was a shriveled fellow in work pants and a dark sweatshirt. The sweatshirt's hood was hanging loose, but he hadn't been doing any running. He looked eighty. What he was holding was a rolled newspaper. He lowered it. "Like to have scared the pants off me," he said in a rusty voice.

"Sorry."

"No one s'posed to be down here but me."

I told him what had brought me, told him I'd been on the campus the other day. He peered into the surrounding shadows and rubbed his mouth. "Ain't seen no one. I stepped out to get the paper. You think he come down here?"

I shrugged. "The door's unlocked. Does this lead anywhere?"

"It's old steam tunnels that hook up to the older buildings on campus. Ain't been used in years." He sent an uncertain frown into the darkness. "I better call campus security."

We moved around the boiler into the faint glow of another bulb. The space was set up like a tiny office. The man tossed his newspaper onto a table and used an old rotary phone.

I looked at a small plastic Christmas tree and some stuffed animals and assorted chipped coffee mugs. On the wall above the table hung a four-year-old calendar and some AA bumper stickers. There was a Philco radio that might have been plugged into the year it was made: Johnnie Ray was singing "The Little White Cloud That Cried." Overloading the same outlet were a hot plate and a dusty fan. The place was a pack rat's nest. Most of the stuff looked scrounged.

"They'll check out Alum Hall and swing by here," the man said, hanging up the phone. "Hey, Curtis Smyth, by the way. With a 'y,' but it's still pronounced 'Smith,' not like some folks like to say Smyth, make it sound like 'sm*i*le'—to be different, I guess." We shook hands, and he turned the radio down beyond hearing. "Started out sweeping floors. I mind this baby now." He nodded at the boiler. "I'm hung out to dry is the truth of it. A friend of Bill's. Ten years now, but I still think about it. Still know the smell of it." He looked at me meaningfully, then laughed. "Hey, live and let live. I'm not bein' hospitable. Want coffee?"

"No, thanks."

"Yeah, it's kinda late. I lose track down here. My own little world. I like the warmth for my arther-itus. Boiler's old, but good. A Scannell, built right here in the city."

As if in agreement, the motor grumbled to life. Curtis Smyth fished something from the pocket of his sweatshirt and looked at it in the light. It was a short piece of metal tube with copper wire wrapped around it. "Found this little wingdoodle on the floor," he said. "Always more than one use for anything." He set it in a soap dish next to the Philco. "Hey," he said, "I see in the paper Jerry Corbin's makin' a return."

"Do you go back that far?"

"Oh, hell, yes. And then some. One day at a time."

"Did you know Corbin when he was here?"

He gave a silent laugh. "They'll be comin' outta the woodwork now, sayin' they was his roommate or his best friend's sister. Have a sit." He waved me into a bentwood chair that Clyde Beatty might have used to hold off tigers. Smyth sank into an easy chair, making the cracked vinyl sigh. "I never knew him personal, but he was noticeable when he was here. In this club, on that team. Big, good-lookin' Irish kid, had been in the service. Smart as a whip, too. He was on the debate club, as I recollect, and on TV. Seems to me that had something to do with Corbin gettin' his break in show business. Back in the days of Jack Paar and them. Before your time."

"God bless you," I said.

"Prof Westrake was his coach. For a while there, Jerry was Prof's protocol"—he frowned—"that the word I want? I used to sweep the old humanities building, and young Corbin'd be hangin' around the office Westrake and his missus shared. She was a prof, too. Corbin was always around. If I didn't know better . . ." He broke off and squinted up at the light bulb, as though to illuminate his memory, but I couldn't see how it would do much.

"You'd say what?" I prompted.

He shook his head. "Nah. Just thinkin' aloud, and not much good at that. Live and let live. 'Protégé.' That's the word I meant, what Jerry was to the prof. Anyways, I'll go see Corbin's show when he comes. I won't be on any VIP list, I guess—though I could probably sneak up to the auditorium through the tunnels." He turned to peer into the dim maze beyond us. "But I'll scrounge the dough and probably go. Hell of a comedian, Jerry Corbin. Last of the breed."

I told Curtis Smyth that if he saw anything of interest, I'd appreciate a call. I gave him one of my cards. I didn't bother with the spelling change; unless someone was writing a check, I saw no need. He said, "Sure thing," and carefully set the card on the ledge by the Philco and the little scrap of wire and tubing he'd found; one more knickknack for the pile. He could always pick his teeth with a corner.

9

WHEN I WOKE up Wednesday morning, the cavalry had been in overnight and used my tongue as a boot scraper. As the coffee perked, I opened a bagel without slicing off any fingers and wedged it into the toaster to burn while I took a shower. At 9:00, half-awake at least, I phoned the Riverfront Plaza and was told that the Corbin entourage had already decamped for rehearsals at the university. There was a message asking me to get over there and look for Justin Ross when I did.

On campus there was a little more excitement than usual, students milling about outside the auditorium, where *The New Gong Show* rehearsals were being held. Jerry Corbin's name was in the air. As I went through the lobby, no one mistook me for a star.

Gripaldi was inside, as inconspicuous as a '58 Edsel. "Yo, Mr. R.!" he greeted me. When I raised my arms for a frisk, he grinned.

"I'm looking for Justin Ross," I said. "Seen him?"

"Down front there a while ago. Mr. C.'s got everyone hopping."

The auditorium was dark, except for the stage. Up there some of the lights in the overhead grid were on, bathing a cluster of about a dozen people in their glow. I didn't see Ross, but Jerry Corbin was evident. Gone was the pouchy softness of the night before. He looked so refreshed that I wondered if he was a stand-in. I took the other people to be the production crew. There was a powwow in progress, with Corbin clearly the chief. Chelsea Nash stood by with her clipboard, taking notes. She had a healthy glow, too. Maybe I should go up and bask in the light for a while. To one side, near the foot of the stage stairs, I spotted Morrie. He was parked at a table, munching a doughnut as he poked his calculator. He didn't look any better at all. I went over.

"How's the getting and spending going?" I said.

He glared up at me. "Jerry's financial affairs are none of your goddamn business."

"And don't forget it," I said. "Justin Ross around?"

Morrie gestured in the vicinity of backstage. I climbed the stairs and moved around the curtain. There was a narrow corridor there, with several closed doors off it. One door at the far end was open. As I neared the door, I heard Ross's raised voice. "Is that some kind of *threat?*" he was saying.

I stepped to where I could look in and see him and stopped. He was standing in profile in a wash of spotlight, garbed in jeans, a tan leather vest over a denim shirt, and his ostrich-hide boots, and for an instant I thought he was rehearsing lines. Then another voice came from among some stage props painted to look like marble columns. "It's a caution. He'd be wise to be careful."

The voice was reedy and used up: an old man's voice.

"Or what?" Ross said.

"He ought to keep his mouth shut. Those are not people who are going to stand for being the brunt of a joke forever."

"In case you're so absentminded you've forgotten," Ross said, "free speech isn't limited to academics."

"Free speech! Free *rein* around here, it looks like!" Because of the props, I couldn't see the other speaker well; only a dim form, gesturing there in the shadows. "I'm going to let the dean know my displeasure." I heard him stalk off.

"Be my guest. Hell, phone the newspapers!" Ross called after him. "Just spell the *names* right!"

A door slammed. I waited a moment before I went in. Ross looked up. "Rasmussen."

"R-a-s-m-u-s-s-e-n," I said.

He frowned. "You catch that?"

"Some."

"He got the word that a play he's rehearsing—some version of *Hamlet*—has been bumped to another location."

"Who is he?"

"Name's Westrake."

I glanced beyond the thicket of prop columns. "Professor Westrake?"

"We need the space, and the university knows the exposure will be good." Ross stopped. "Yeah, that's him. You know him?"

"Heard the name. He was Jerry's teacher, wasn't he?"

Ross seemed surprised that I knew it. "What was he lecturing about?" I asked.

"Harvard. Jerry's got that shtick he does. Harvard, the Eastern establishment, Ivy Leaguers. Easy targets because WASPs don't fight back. Their idea of anger is to not offer you cocktails."

"I'm glad I don't know many."

"Westrake was telling me Jerry should drop it. I may have been a bit rough on the old dude. I'm jumpy this morning." He adjusted the silver longhorn steer slide on his bolo tie. "Have you spoken to Jerry yet?"

"No."

Ross took an envelope from his shirt pocket and handed it to me. It had Corbin's name hand-lettered on it. Inside was a small pasteboard skeleton, its jointed arms and legs folded in. I swung them open. A face had been glued on the skull—from a picture of a young Jerry Corbin. On the back of the skeleton someone had written: *It tolls for thee.*

I glanced at Ross. He didn't look so good; one day in New England and his tan was already fading. Maybe we should both go stand under the stage lights.

"It was at the hotel desk this morning, left there in a bunch of flowers late last night. Nobody saw who delivered them."

"Probably some little guy with wings on his feet," I said. "At the risk of sounding boring, is Corbin still resistant to telling the cops?"

"You're kidding, right? You know how much work has gone into this show? We're two days away. The boat's launched. Spring a small leak now, we start shipping water, the whole schmear could go down like the Titanic."

"Nice extended metaphor," I said. "You just come up with that?"

"Goddammit, Rasmussen. This isn't a joke."

"I know."

"That's number four, for chrissakes."

"Yeah." I was feeling pressed. Whoever was sending messages was at close range now. A net was tightening, but it wasn't mine. The only people who weren't potential suspects were over in Westlawn Cemetery. Maybe I was better suited for shadowing people on aluminum walkers, though even they were getting friskier lately. "Can I hang onto this?" I said.

"Go ahead."

Just then a thin young man came in. He nodded at us and went over to the props and began lifting one of the stage columns. His hair was cropped close on the sides and went up and fanned out on top like a typewriter eraser. Balancing a pair of columns on his shoulders, he went out. I said to Ross, "Is this what you wanted to see me about?"

"I want us to have a skull session with Jerry. He's lunching with reporters, so I don't want to screw that up, or afternoon rehearsal. How about tonight at the hotel. Seven-thirty?" I said okay. "I hope you can come up with some answers by then," Ross said.

I told him I'd give it the old college try. As I started out, he said, "Rasmussen."

I turned.

"We've got a crew on this show, a lot of people doing a lot of jobs. Folks alive in the business."

"Translate," I said.

"You've probably seen all the Jerry stuff in the tabloids. I know he comes off as a blowhard at times. But he genuinely cares about what he does, and about people. He's a good guy, and he deserves some luck. I think the network's getting ready to hang him out to dry on *Good Night.*"

"Cancel him?"

"Some of his West Coast staff are already papering the town with their résumés. So this new show means everything. It's a chance for . . . I don't know, redemption? If it blows up before Saturday night, if anything—bad press, news leak—if something stops the show . . . it'll be the kiss of death for all of us."

Skull session; blows up; kiss of death. I hoped Ross's images were accidental.

10

I OVERTOOK THE young man carrying the stage props and offered him a hand. He gave me a Doric column. I asked him if he was in Professor Westrake's play.

"Just a stagehand," he said. We went out a side door and started across a sunny quadrangle. "Unfortunately the play just got bumped. Prof isn't a happy camper right now."

"On account of Jerry Corbin's show?"

"I think so. I think he and Mr. Corbin have bad blood between them."

"Really?" I said it casually. I didn't want to scare him off.

"Prof used to have Mr. Corbin as a student, so I asked him about it, and he basically told me mind my own business and concentrate on the play."

We went into another building and deposited the props in a small lecture hall. "Is Professor Westrake around now?" I asked.

"Probably in his office," the kid said. "Bitching."

The muted rings from the campus bell tolling 11:00 drifted through the trees as I climbed the steps to Canterbury Hall. A directory in the foyer sent me up two more flights. Canterbury was the humanities building, one of the older structures on campus, all varnished wood, shadowed linoleum, and the feeling of time. As I neared Room 313, I smelled cigars. Apparently the smoke-free-workplace idea hadn't made it up this far yet. Alfred Westrake's name, with PROFESSOR EMERITUS under it, was painted on the pebbled glass panel of the wooden door, which stood open. Inside, a man with long white hair drawn into a ponytail sat at the desk. He had his back to me and was staring out a window.

"Professor Westrake?"

He turned a gaunt face on me, with deep-set eyes and thick, unruly eyebrows that curled at the tops of his gold-frame glasses like honeysuckle overrunning a trellis. I guessed him to be seventy-five. "What?" he said.

"My name is Rasmussen. I'd like to talk if you have a few minutes."

"If it's about tryouts for *A Christmas Carol,* you're a month early," he said in the voice I'd heard arguing with Justin Ross.

"It's about next weekend."

"Next weekend? Goddammit, this is our tenth rehearsal. We've got exactly five days until opening." He frowned. "Are you a student? You look kind of old."

I let it pass. "I'm a private investigator."

The frown deepened. "And you want to talk about *Traitorous Gifts?*"

"What's that?"

"My play. What are you here for?"

"I thought you were doing *Hamlet.*"

"What is it you want?" he said.

"To talk about Jerry Corbin."

"Corbin? Are you after him?"

"Figuratively, I guess I am. Mind if I sit down?"

He sighed. "You may as well. We're not getting anywhere *this* way."

I took a wooden chair by the desk. Like everything else in the room, it was old, worn to a curvy shine by generations of student rear ends. The office was narrowed by crowded bookshelves. The one wall not dominated by them had the window in it, flanking which was an array of framed photographs. They gave an impression of smaller windows that looked into an indefinite past. I said, "Corbin hired me to look out for him while he's here in Lowell."

"A bodyguard? Is he in danger?"

"I hope not."

Westrake sized me up, whether with newfound respect or scorn, I couldn't tell. "Well, you certainly look as if you would be good at that sort of thing."

"I'm trying to get some background from people who know Corbin."

"Cross me off the list. I haven't spoken with him in ages."

Westrake took a stub of evil-looking black cigar from an ashtray and produced a silver lighter.

"Can you do that in here?" I asked.

"Do what?"

Flame danced and died in his eyeglasses. The lighter snapped shut. "When I knew Jerry Corbin, he was a young man—bright enough, curious, though not very focused. He spread himself thin."

"On what?" I asked.

"Drama, debate, sports, whatever was going on. Coeds. He was attending on the G.I. Bill, probably simply for something to do. It worked, I suppose. There's no denying he's made a name for himself."

"The university is giving him an honorary degree, I hear."

Westrake blew smoke at the ceiling. "Not through any fault of mine. I mean, it isn't as if he were in legitimate theater."

"Shakespeare?" I said.

"Look, Mr.—"

"Rasmussen."

"—we all were taken by young Jeremiah Corbin." For an

instant, I thought he'd said taken *in.* "He was popular, and we were close during his last few semesters—even friends, to a point. But after his graduation he turned his back on all that. He had gone to California for a screen test. He possessed a certain Hibernian sparkle that came across on the little video box, and some smart cookie out there saw it. I guess we know the rest." He spoke as though each word burned his tongue. With a glance at me from under his tangled brows, he shifted forward in his chair. "I felt betrayed. I'd coached him in classical acting and debate, taken him under my wing. Though why I should have expected any different, I don't know. It's just that he had real curiosity. In my experience, it's rare." Westrake waved at the smoke as though freeing himself of the past's pull and sat back. "Ah, who cares? As I said, that was long ago."

"Not a big Corbin fan, huh?"

"You can get annoying with all those questions."

"My Socratic training," I said.

His brows crinkled skeptically. "Socrates?"

"He's my favorite ancient philosopher, after Barney Rubble."

Westrake stubbed out the cigar. "I give Corbin his due. The man is a household name. That's an achievement of a sort, I suppose. But pop culture weighed against all this tradition?" His glance took in the rows of books. "Ah, it's humbug. I won't be bothered by this Gong Show silliness. For me personally, his being here is an inconvenience. I've got a play to put on. Not *Hamlet,* in answer to your question. *Traitorous Gifts*. I've adapted Shakespeare. Two acts, fewer characters—but the heart is still beating, I hope. I was counting on the use of that auditorium. Instead they've consigned me to a broom closet. But I'll make do. And now, sir, if there's nothing more—"

I took a chance and said, "I overheard your run-in with Corbin's assistant."

"That one. What is he supposed to be, some sort of cowboy? He was out of line."

"He says you think Corbin should change his jokes."

"I do. Corbin has been lampooning Harvard on national television for years. He goes too far. He should be careful, get some new material."

"Why Harvard?" I asked. "I haven't figured that out."

He frowned at me. "You don't know the genesis of that?"

"It wasn't in the press kit."

Westrake said nothing for a moment. Beyond the office window, the campus blazed with autumn. Finally he said, "In the fifties there was a television quiz show which pitted colleges against one another for scholarship money. Matches were held regionally, with victors advancing through several rounds for a chance to compete nationally. I assembled a team here, and we entered. We did well, and we drew Harvard for the regional finals. When that was announced, it got a lot of interest. Bear in mind, in those days, we were a parochial little teachers' college. Harvard must have seen it that way as well. Perhaps they didn't take the challenge seriously enough. As it turned out, we beat them. Only a few points, but it didn't matter. It was a stunning upset. A team of state-school kids overcoming Ivy League bluebloods."

He reached and lifted one of the old photographs from the wall near his desk and handed it to me. "That's us."

There were six people in the photo, one of them a crew-cut Jerry Corbin. The names were printed underneath. With Corbin, similarly dressed in blazers with a college patch on the pocket, were three other young men, a young woman identified as Flo Ryan, and Westrake, without the long hair. He said, "I selected Jeremiah over more purely intellectual students because he was a cool customer. I felt he would be able to deliver under pressure. And here"—he took down a second photograph—"was the foursome we vanquished."

He waited until I finished jotting the names from both photos into my notebook before he asked why. I shrugged. "I'm in information management, just like everyone else."

When he had replaced the photographs on his wall, he said, "People labor under the delusion that one more fact, one added bit of data, and the world is going to crack open for them like an oyster. It's a myth. You have to grasp the underlying principles to get any place in this life."

"Probably," I said, "but I'm a creature of habit. Of course, I haven't gotten anyplace."

I drove down to the city library and did some digging in the microfilm collection. Alfred Westrake had been understating it when he said that the local college's win over Harvard had got some notice. Photographs in the *Sun* showed downtown sidewalks deep with celebrants as Lowell welcomed the team back from New York City. The losing squad, by contrast, had cried sour grapes, the account stated, with someone from Harvard protesting "irregularities" in the show's format. The irregularities weren't spelled out. One file photo I came across showed Alfred Westrake and a youthful Jeremiah Corbin, both in tuxedos, clenching cigars in their grinning mouths. Something about the picture struck me, and I pondered that for a moment, then knew what it was. I took out the envelope Ross had given me and drew out the little pasteboard skeleton. The face glued to it wasn't identical to the one in the file photo, but it clearly had been taken around the same time, perhaps on the same occasion. So?

Okay, I had a few more bits of data. I sat for a moment trying to grasp some underlying principle. Then I gave up and left.

11

WHEN I GOT to my office shortly past noon, I phoned police headquarters. The desk officer put me through to Ed St. Onge.

"What are you doing?" I said.

"Tending my orchids. What do you want?"

I gave him the names of Corbin's teammates from the quiz team. "I'm curious to know if any of them has been in trouble."

"Who are they?"

"Thirty years ago, they were college students."

"What the hell? Is this what Mr. Good Night America has you doing for him?"

"You've got this fixation with Corbin," I said. "From what I read in the tabloids, he's not the marrying kind; but if you're extra good, maybe I can get you an autographed eight-by-ten."

"Don't shit me. I hope it doesn't end up I'm *taking* his picture."

I was silent.

"No snappy reply for that one, do you. Well, I heard from All Saints this morning. The woman who was attacked over at the university is on the mend. Guess whose name came up?"

"What did she say?"

"I haven't heard her say anything yet, but her husband has been in. Turns out one of *her* classmates was Jerry Corbin. Small world."

"Do you know what her name was back then?" I asked.

"As a matter of fact I do."

"Was it Flo Ryan?"

"Then what're you asking me for?" he growled.

As I hung up the phone, the paralegal from the office down the hall came by for take-out orders for lunch. I put in my request, then sat back to think. On a pad I jotted words randomly, clustering them the way I'd seen a creativity consultant do on TV. Supposed to help you find hidden links between ideas. Maybe I could even find an underlying principle or two. I could use some. One word that came up several times was *college.* Alfred Westrake had been Corbin's professor, and Florence Murphy his classmate. I dug out my notebook and thumbed to the notes I had taken an hour ago. Flo *Ryan*—now Murphy—had been on the quiz-bowl team with Corbin. That got a couple question marks. The university was where I had first seen Chelsea Nash. Then there was Harvard—as in losing team, the butt of Corbin's jokes, the meat of Westrake's warning, lodgers of a protest over their loss to Lowell, situated in Cambridge, where note number three had been mailed. More question marks.

Meanwhile, St. Onge's crack about taking Corbin's picture nettled me. I didn't want to think about crime-scene photos. But I had to wonder: was I doing the job? When I met with Corbin that night, I wanted something to hand him that said yes. So far, I seemed to be dealing with people and events from three decades ago. I needed to gather more facts.

The demographers kept insisting that the northeast was losing bodies to the Sunbelt, but no one had told the greater Boston phone book. It clumped on my desk like a cinder block. I checked the listings for Harvard, which filled more pages than most Arizona towns. I found the department I wanted and dialed.

"Office of Alumni Affairs," intoned a vintage telephone voice. "Ms. Bishop speaking."

I gave my name. "I'm trying to get information on four men who would have been at Harvard in the late fifties, early sixties," I said. "If I provide names, would it be possible for you to get me current addresses?"

"Why do you need that information, Mr. Rasmussen?"

I could hand her the truth and maybe get shot down outright, or try something else. "I represent UMass Lowell," I said. "We're planning to honor our quiz-bowl team from long ago which, ahem, beat Harvard? The men I'm seeking were the Harvard team. We want to do a puff piece—'how-soon-we-forget, where-are-they-now?' All in good fun, of course."

"I see. Well, you'd have to speak with Mr. Stahl, the director."

"Could I do that?"

"Just a moment, please," Ms. Bishop said.

She dumped me into a musical hold pattern. "Uptown Girl." The paralegal brought my sandwich and I paid her. I reread the names I had jotted in Professor Westrake's office. The music went on. I thought Ms. Bishop had forgotten me. I was getting ready to hang up when she came back. "Mr. Rasmussen, are you still there?"

"Just me and Billy Joel," I said.

I think her laugh was throaty. "I got hold of Mr. Stahl. He's on his way to a luncheon meeting. May I have him return your call?"

I supposed I could sit there for a spell and answer my phone, "Good afternoon, University of Massachusetts at Lowell Publicity Office . . ." I glanced at the Italian sandwich oozing grease through the wax wrapper in front of me. "Actually, I'm about to take a lunch meeting myself, but I'm going to be in your area this afternoon. Would it be convenient if I came by in person?"

"Um, all right, sure. If you want to."

We settled on 3:00. She told me to come to Wadsworth House, opposite the Holyoke Center in Harvard Square, and ask for her—Ms. Bishop. She would get me to Mr. Stahl.

* * *

In the movies, the guy shows up in doctor's whites and strolls past police guards to get at the surviving witness. I carried a dozen roses from the hospital gift shop. At the nurses' station on the third floor, I identified myself as a visitor for Florence Murphy.

Standing outside the hospital-room door was Gus Deemys. He pushed away from the wall when he saw me.

"Well, what do you know," he said. "It's Coin-op. Back to finish the job?" He had on an olive suit, a matching shirt, and a bright yellow tie.

"Hi, Gus," I said. "Nice getup. I didn't know the racetracks were open."

St. Onge appeared in the doorway. "Forget it," he said.

"Ain't he a riot?" Deemys said. "They get funnier every year, don't they, Ed? Another ten years, I might even smile."

"Inside, Gus," St. Onge ordered.

Deemys blinked. "What?"

"Rasmussen—with me."

We strolled down the corridor a distance and stopped. Folding his arms across five-inch lapels, St. Onge leaned against the glazed-block wall. "So?"

"I figure I've got a stake in how she's doing."

"Yeah? I don't. But maybe we can do this tougher. Maybe you're a threat to my witness."

I looked at him. His hard dark eyes didn't flicker. "Convince me," he said.

It wasn't going to end unless one of us waved a flag. I said, "You already know who my client is, and that he and Florence Murphy were classmates. He's been getting weird notes lately."

"Kind of weird notes? Threats?"

"Not exactly. But they've got a crazy tone. It could be just a sick joke."

"Or a stalker," St. Onge said. "That what you're saying?"

"I'm trying to find out. But Corbin doesn't want bad press."

"He won't get it from me."

"Maybe what happened to Florence Murphy has a connection. I'd like to ask her a few questions."

"Whose were those names you gave me?"

"More classmates. They were on a quiz team together."

"And you're playing Sherlock Holmes."

I shrugged. "Eliminating the impossible."

St. Onge chewed his mustache a moment. "The woman's out of danger, but she's still foggy. I can't let you in. Suppose though—" He broke off to watch a cluster of nurses walk by. Their uniforms were a rainbow of colors. "None of them wear white anymore," Ed said.

"Deregulation."

"I like nurses in white, nuns in black."

"And cops in blue," I said. "Suppose what?"

He sent a last look at the departing nurses. "You're the one who got the medics in fast. Her doctors say that was important. Maybe when she comes around more fully, she'll look kindly on it."

"And want to reward me?"

"She could remember something important."

I nodded. "All right. Thanks." I gave him the roses. "For her. Let me know."

12

IT TOOK ME forty minutes to reach Harvard Square and ten more of cruising before I gave up on finding street parking and stashed the car in a multi-tier garage that had sprouted since I was there last. There had been a time when my former wife and I had been regulars in the square. Lauren was finishing a degree at Lesley. I would drive in to meet her after my shifts on the cops, and we'd hang out. The best places were the hole-in-the-wall bars, the ratty bookstores, and the basement cafés. Our favorite was the Algiers. For the price of a cup of coffee, you could sit for hours in the dim room, amid the waft of Gauloise smoke from adjoining tables, and talk. Didn't matter what: Sartre or laundry soap, it all took on a weight of Left Bank seriousness. Ah, youth!

But Harvard Square had changed. The funk had fled south to Central Square, the old places yanked out like bad teeth, replaced with gleaming edifices of steel and glass. It was an economy of scale, and cash always tipped the balance away from charm. What once had been a crossroads where Nobel laureates mingled with backpack poets, and tourists from Altoona crossed paths with Dinka tribesmen, was different now. It glittered and sang and made cash registers ring, but it would always be a second-rate Rodeo Drive. Ah, middle age.

For the college that surrounded it and gave it its name, *old* was measured in red brick and centuries. Holyoke Center was definitely *new* Harvard: ten floors of prestressed concrete with bright shops at the street level, and not an ivy leaf in sight. I passed through the concourse and crossed Mass Avenue to Wadsworth House, a yellow wood-frame where, according to a faded sign, George Washington had once resided. I climbed to the second floor.

The engraved-plastic name plate on Ms. Bishop's desk actually said "Ms." She was a trim forty, with crisp dark hair and a spray of tiny freckles across her nose. Seeing me, she sat back, framed me with her hands, and narrowed one gray eye. I squared my shoulders.

"Love your chapeau," she said. "That's high camp."

I took it off, and shaped it, and said, "Around here, maybe. Where I come from, no one's ever quit wearing them long enough for them to become a fashion statement."

Her laugh *was* throaty. "I'm in love with old cinema, when every woman wore a pinch-waist dress and every man a suit and hat."

"And they all smoked Luckies," I said.

She made a face. "Just give me the dark suit and fedora and that film-noir feel."

I shrugged. "What can I say? I'm a film-noir kind of guy." I gave my name.

"No kidding? You don't look the academic type."

I thought about it a second, then decided to confess. I had no reason to blacken the name of UMass. I gave her one of my cards. She read it with a raised brow. "That was a pretty bold lie," she said.

"But I'm as honest as the day is long once I get my foot in the door."

"Do you do that often?"

"Get in the door?"

"Make up stories on the telephone."

"Happens mostly when Channel 56 is rerunning *The Rockford Files.*"

Ms. Bishop's smile was a sparkler. "Well, have a seat. May I keep this?"

She slipped my card into her blouse pocket, then pointed at a door covered with crimson leather studded with brass tacks. "If I'm to get you past *that* door, I'm going to have to know the true story. Mr. Stahl is class of sixty-seven, B.A. in management, and strictly business."

"A person I'm working for once appeared on a TV quiz show on which the men I'm interested in were also contestants. I'm trying to backtrack to see if any of the men have been in touch with my client lately."

"Wouldn't your client know that?"

"Not if the contact was made anonymously."

"Hmm. Sounds sinister. Is there a crime involved?"

"Not that I know of," I said.

"And Lowell really beat Harvard?"

"So I'm told."

She seemed to find the fact impressive. "Well, forewarned is forearmed. Mr. Stahl is protective of alums. Of course, he *does* manage to relieve them of the burden of several millions of dollars in gifts and donations each year."

I nodded sympathetically. "That's a heavy burden. Tell me, will I have to untangle my lie with him?"

"You're in luck. We're getting ready to begin our fall telephone canvass, so he's just back from a strategy session. I haven't done anything yet but write your name on his calendar. But I spelled it differently than on your card."

"Good for you. That's a printer's error."

"And you let them get away with it?"

"They're a small operation, and so am I. And this way, maybe people remember me."

She smiled again. "I started remembering you the minute you walked in."

The intercom on her desk buzzed. "Is my three o'clock here yet, Ms. Bishop?" piped a brisk voice. "Mr. Rasmussen?"

She looked at me. "Yes, sir. I'll send him in."

She pointed a finger at the leather-clad door.

Mr. Stahl was standing beside a big cherrywood desk reading a report. On a wall behind him was a pair of lacrosse sticks, or racquets, or whatever they called them. There was also a poster that said: NOTHING IS FOREVER EXCEPT DEATH, TAXES, AND HARVARD. He glanced at me over half-frame tortoiseshell glasses, then put the report down and came over, hand extended.

"Bart Stahl," he said. "Class of sixty-seven." His cheeks were shiny with a shave that looked ten minutes old, and there was high wattage in his smile.

I smiled back. "My name's Rasmussen, Mr. Stahl. No class at all. I'm a private investigator."

The smile did a brownout, then dimmed altogether when I handed him my license.

He was medium height, with sandy hair combed the way it would have been in his yearbook picture. He had on a herringbone tweed jacket with a white oxford button-down shirt and a red club tie, gray wool slacks, argyle socks and brown Weejuns. There was a class ring on his hand that could dent a Saab. He would have chuckled at the primitive ritual of motorcycle club members wearing their colors. He gave back the license.

"What was it you wanted, Mr. Rasmussen?"

"I'm hoping to get some current information on several alums."

When I had laid it out in brief for him, he frowned, cleared his throat, and said, "I see." I had the feeling he was getting ready to give me the Ivy League version of the bum's rush. "I had assumed that this was college business," he said, "that perhaps you had attended Harvard yourself."

"I once spent a fair amount of effort trying to make a young woman think so," I said.

"Well, I'll be direct. While it may be true that we are not talking about state secrets here, I do feel sufficient uncertainty about your request to make me hesitant. Furthermore, I'm not sure I like the precedent this might set. Therefore, I'm going to exercise my discretion and decline."

"That wasn't *that* direct," I said.

He didn't smile. "I don't want to have to call campus security."

"All right. You don't have to throw in the combination to the office safe."

He picked up his telephone. There was a cherrywood chair in front of the desk, with the college emblem and *Veritas* stenciled in gold on the back. I sat in it. His hand hung frozen with the phone in it. I leaned forward and set my hat on the edge of his desk. He hesitated a few seconds, maybe wishing he could lay one of the lacrosse sticks across my skull. Then he hung up the phone. "Look," I said, "I'm not in the business of being indiscreet. In fact, just the basic information can probably clear up any questions I have, and I'll be on my merry way."

He went behind his desk and sat in his own chair. He cleared his throat again. "Our alumni organization is the finest in the world. We've got more than a quarter of a million members. We have a responsibility to them."

Keep those checks and endowments coming, I thought. I said, "Understood. I'll tell you what. I'll give you the names, you tell me addresses, without mentioning whose is whose, and if I can rule out any of them on that basis, I will."

He sighed. I wrote out the four names, and he called in Ms. Bishop and gave her the list. "Jacket data only," he instructed.

When she had gone, he swiveled his chair to face away from me at an angle. From a sideboard he took a briar pipe, clopped it loudly in his palm, stuffed the bowl with Leavitt and Peirce Cake Box and applied a match. The aroma was a lot sweeter than Westrake's cigar. Ms. Bishop returned in a few minutes and handed him a sheet of printer paper. She moved gracefully, as if she was being careful not to disturb the smoke. As she turned to go, she gave me a surreptitious wink. I liked the way it crinkled the freckles across her nose.

"Okay," Stahl said when he had replaced his half-frames, "we've got one in Yakima, Washington." He glanced at me, looking for reaction. "Another in Brussels, Belgium. Like the first, he's been there for more than a decade."

"Is anyone still in the Boston area?"

"One of them lived here in Cambridge . . . before he passed away two summers ago."

"And the other?"

"The other lives in Cohasset."

It was on the South Shore, twenty miles from Boston. I glanced at the names in my notebook and took a shot. "Ralph Tatum."

Stahl set down his pipe. "I don't know if I want to take this any further."

"You'll be saving me time, is all. I can check all four names in the directory."

"Pickering. Noel Pickering. One-forty-four Jerusalem Road."

"Thank you."

In the outer office, I leaned close to Ms. Bishop's desk and asked quietly, "Is that *Ms.* a miss or missus?"

"Part of your private investigation?"

"Lively curiosity," I said.

"It's the former."

"As in the former *Mrs.* Bishop?"

"As in not latter. I'm single." She smiled. "First name's Judy."

"Hi, Judy," I said. I put on my hat, gunned her with a finger pistol and walked through the door.

Outside, sycamore leaves spun on the sidewalk, chasing

scraps of *Barron's* and flyers for dulcimer lessons. I found a phone booth and made a call. I looked at my watch. Almost 3:30. If I hustled I could get into the front wedge of southbound traffic. There was a Cohasset exit off Route 3.

13

ADD CYPRESS TREES and Japanese golfers, and Cohasset could be Monterey East. Jerusalem Road gave rugged ocean views as it twisted along the rocky shore. The homes were a mishmash of styles, with the only thing in common being that they were expensive. I almost missed the mailbox with 144 on it. I backed up to where I could peer past a rustic wooden fence.

The Pickering house was smaller than most, a cedar-shingled Cape Cod with an ell, weathered silver and grown with vines that would have bloomed with color in June but were only a net of crisp leaves now. I pulled into the crushed-shell driveway, parked behind an old station wagon and a white Lexus, and got out. It was 5:00. I stretched and replaced the fumes in my lungs with salt air. The sea and sky were blue, and gulls cried over the foamy inlet below. The commute from the city would be a bitch, but once you were here, life would be worth every mile.

The front door was fashioned from oak planks and set in a low frame. I didn't need to knock. A woman approached from the side yard. She had on work gloves, a cell phone in one hand and a gardening spade in the other. "Hi," she said. "I'm mulching the iris beds. If only this weather would last!"

"It never does," I said. "Mrs. Pickering?"

"Yes. Mr. Rasmussen?"

I said I was. We had spoken briefly on the phone through a bad connection, and I realized now she probably had been talking from her garden. She was a pretty woman, tall and slender, with eyes of the same soft blue as her velour sweat suit. She pushed back a spray of ash gold hair with her wrist. "Come on in."

I needed to duck to get through the front door. I followed Mrs. Pickering through several low-ceilinged rooms into a large, well-equipped kitchen. She set the phone in its cradle and offered me coffee, then gave me a hand-thrown ceramic mug to hold while she poured from a vacuum carafe.

"I'm Missy, by the way."

"Alex," I said.

I had gotten the phone number from directory assistance and called from Cambridge. Through the static, Mrs. Pickering had told me that Noel was working but would be done at 5:00. I said I'd drive down.

I guessed Missy Pickering to be fifty, give or take a few years. Hers was the kind of bred beauty that ages well. Like the house. It was an antique, restored and furnished in what I took to be authentic style, if you didn't deduct points for the kitchen gizmos.

"Noel will be done just about now," she said. "He's precise about his schedule. Bring your coffee." She led me into the ell at the rear of the kitchen. "This weekend the clocks go back, and he frets all winter about losing the good north light."

I was slow grabbing that. "He's a painter?" I asked as we stepped into a small backyard.

She turned to look at me, her forehead crinkling with fine lines. "You don't know him?"

"We've never met," I said. "I'm a private investigator from Lowell."

"Goodness, I thought . . . Well, it wasn't clear on the phone. He knows some Rasmussens. An investigator. Is anything wrong?"

"I just want to ask him a few questions about someone else he may know."

She hesitated, uncertain all at once, maybe sorry her good breeding had made her so hospitable. "Well, he's out here."

In the backyard was a shed perched near the edge of the drop-off to the inlet below. I could hear the ocean as we walked out. Missy Pickering opened a door and called in, "Noel, Mr. Rasmussen is here. He's a private investigator." She said to me, "Go right in."

As she retreated to the house, I stepped into the shed. Against a huge window, a tall man stood in silhouette before an easel. He was wiping brushes with a cloth and paid no attention to me. I didn't mind. On two of the walls hung a lot of unframed canvases, bright in the incoming light. They were seascapes mostly, depicting the view beyond the big window in an array of moods. The paintings were good.

The man at the easel came over now. He had on a backyard chef's apron, from the paint-streaked front of which Paul Prudhomme eyed me; or was it Dom DeLuise?

"Hi. Noel Pickering," he said in a voice more suited to a clap on the back than the almost-delicate handshake he offered. His hand left a scent of turpentine on mine. He was my height, with a slight stoop—probably from going in and out of his front door—and sandy hair flecked with white. Like his wife, he would be good-looking all his days.

"These are good," I said, indicating the seascapes on the walls. "Working on a new one?"

He smiled. "Come have a look."

I did—and felt my body tighten. I was staring into someone's sliced-open stomach. The painting was full-size, in living color on canvas board. The viscera seemed to glisten and throb. I know mine did.

"That stuff on the walls is my first love," Pickering said. "But I can't *give* it away—or just barely. This is my bread and butter."

"People buy this?" I said.

He laughed. "Medical texts. I'm an illustrator. I work from photographs. And memory. I was a general surgeon for twenty years. I see Missy offered coffee. Would you care for something sneaky in it?"

"As long as it isn't paint thinner," I said.

From an old wooden cabinet he produced a bottle of Jameson's. He refilled a mug of his own from a hot pot and splashed a dollop of whiskey into each of our cups. He lifted his. "What can I do for you, sir?"

I gave him a card, which he looked at and said, "The people I know spell it differently." I did too, but I didn't go into it. Without mentioning Jerry Corbin I laid out a general idea of why I was there. He sipped coffee and listened, and finally said, "So you're wondering if after all these years someone might be trying to even a score by sending scary notes."

"That's about it," I said.

"Exploratory surgery. Hmm." Pickering turned so we were both facing the large window, beyond which daylight was fading on the sea. The colors kept changing. I could see the wink of a lighthouse offshore.

" 'I love you,' " Pickering said abruptly.

"What?"

"The blink pattern. Minot's Ledge light. One, four, three. They call it Lover's Light. Fog bank coming." He pointed. "See it?"

A luminous mist was visible on the southeastern horizon, as if someone had brushed it there with a delicate stroke. I wondered what it would be like to be a painter and know that if you didn't grab something while you could, you might never see it the same way again. Maybe I did know. "Any ideas?" I asked.

Pickering turned. "You've stirred up some memories here. That was a long time ago, but there are parts that are still in focus."

I waited.

"After that last quiz show, the four of us went back to Cronin's—remember that old place? Long gone. Partly we wanted to nurse our wounds—but hey, college, any excuse to get loaded." His smile came and went. "Anyway, this one fellow got a little blabby and started talking about how we should get even."

"With the Lowell team?"

"Frankly, I was surprised that he felt that way. It wasn't the end of the world or anything. I mean, we'd won five or six weeks running, and taken some scholarship money. Even made front page of the *Crimson.* But he was talking himself into something, said we'd been dishonored, that we should redeem ourselves. And he said there was a way—that his club had an oath of allegiance to uphold its and the college's honor if either were ever sullied. Well, okay, so maybe he was thinking about stealing a mascot, or painting *'Veritas'* on their library steps. But he made it sound more . . . ominous."

"How?" I said.

"Well, for one thing . . . are you familiar with Harvard's club system?"

"No sully intended," I said, "but no."

"The college has no fraternities. It has clubs. Delphic, Porcellian, Hasty Pudding. I was in Phoenix myself. People think they're about exclusion, and I suppose in days gone by there were unwritten sanctions—you know, only members who look like us, read WASPs. That's changed. Some people like to believe that the clubs are old-boy networks that hard-wire you straight to seats of power. Right. Basically the clubs are about comradeship, and service. But, that said, there were always rumors of certain . . . secret clubs."

I set my coffee mug gently on the cabinet, not wanting to miss his words.

"They certainly weren't recognized as part of the system,"

he continued. "And their aims tended more toward mischief. Outlaw clubs. I think that's what this fellow was talking about. He was speaking in rather sepulchral tones—if one can be drunk and sepulchral at the same time." Pickering laughed. "We didn't pay much mind."

"Which one of your teammates was this?" I asked.

"I wish I could remember. We'd been pulled together for the sole purpose of a quiz team. A couple of humanities types, an engineer. I was the science guy. Each bright enough in his own fashion, I suppose, but unintegrated. I mean, what do twenty-one-year-olds know? As to whether this fellow pursued it—God, I have no idea. I can't remember his club, either. As I say, many of these things were rumor. After that boozy little breakup at Cronin's I never saw any of those fellows again."

Beyond the big window, the sea and sky had darkened. Noel Pickering said, "Boy, I haven't thought about this in a long time." He drank some coffee and set his cup down. "Come on into the house a moment."

Missy Pickering was at a sink in the kitchen's center island, washing zucchinis. She looked up suddenly, perhaps expecting to see her husband in handcuffs. Pickering said, "Honey, are those old yearbooks still around?"

In the front room he rummaged in a bookcase and brought a volume over to the lamplight and began paging through it. I stood by, watching a man take a stroll down memory lane. He didn't exclaim "Eureka!" but after a moment he turned the book so I could see what he had found. It was opened to a teams-and-clubs section, and there were the four young Harvardians I had first seen on Alfred Westrake's wall. Pickering tapped his finger on one face. "Tom Chapman. He was the engineer, went on to found his own company. Electronics, I think. He's the fellow I told you about."

From the doorway across the room, Missy Pickering said, "Isn't Tom Chapman the one who had the accident a couple years back, Noel? We saw the notice in the alumni bulletin."

"Jesus, that's right. A sailing mishap off Cape Ann." Noel Pickering turned to me. "You can cross Chapman off your list. The poor bastard drowned."

I asked about the other two teammates, but Pickering had little to offer beyond what the Alumni Affairs office had told me. He did say that the notion of them sending the notes seemed very unlikely.

Outside I stood in the dusk for a few moments and watched Minot's Light sending its love note into the gathering fog. Then I headed for the highway.

14

It was past 7:00 when I got back to Lowell. I drove over to the university. Classes were long over for the day, students off in the dining commons, or beginning Hump Day parties; a few might even have been studying. Guessing that emeritus status carried light official duties, I had no logical reason to expect that Professor Westrake would still be in his office. But he was. He was at his desk, reading. He glanced up as I knocked on the open door.

"You're persistent," he said, with only slight surprise.

"You're stealing my lines," I said. I nodded at the extra chair. He shrugged.

He was in a faded work shirt and brown cords. His hair, freed from the ponytail, hung in a pale fringe over the collar. He adjusted his glasses. "Are you here to question me?"

"Just to chat."

"About Jerry Corbin."

"That must be a source of pride," I said. "To have had him as your student."

"I've had thousands of students. What does it amount to? They pass in this dreck." He lifted the page he had been reading, ripped from a spiral notebook. The handwriting looked none too neat. "You try to leave a little something with them. Most take it as their due, and in the end they leave, without so much as a fart or a fare-thee-well."

What did you say to that?

He said, "I've had a dream. I guess you would call it recurrent. In it I'm walking on a city street. Maybe it's Boston. It doesn't matter. I see someone walking toward me and realize she's a former student of mine. Then, as I look around, each of the people passing on this busy sidewalk—every *one*—is a former student. But none of them knows me. They show no recognition whatsoever. I may not even be there. Dreams tell us a lot, don't you think?"

"I never remember any of them long enough to know," I said.

"Well *I* do. And mine tell me that the labor of teaching drama is the most hazardous in the world. Grappling forever with the skepticism of humankind's big minds. There is no certitude in books. There's nothing sure. And with each passing year, the vagaries of the job befuddle you more. Even the basic questions, rather than grow lucid, get more enigmatic."

"I'd guess that emeritus status means you could hang it up for good," I said.

He frowned at the idea. "The only principle I cling to is that no one inherits a life. You work damn hard to *build* one. The past—tradition, the canon—helps."

I said, "What kind of life did Jerry Corbin build?"

"He's *your* client. Wouldn't he be the one to ask?"

"I plan to," I said.

From his shirt pocket Westrake drew out a packet of small black cigars. Fortunately, he didn't offer one. "I started out in the theater as an actor," he said, tamping a cigar on the desk. "I kicked around awhile, but I realized that if I labored a hundred years, the most I was ever going to get to play was Laertes. I was never going to be Hamlet. So I left it and got into teaching. It's steadier work." He looked at me. "Have you ever been a teacher?"

"No," I said.

"It's an emotional roller coaster. The only thing even

remotely like it is doing live theater. There are days when you feel you're a prince among men, and the world is your realm. But there are other days when you leave the classroom, and it's as if you had uncorked the very cask of despair."

I said nothing, waiting for him to go on. He wanted to.

"My wife Anita and I lived near the campus in those days. It was a cozy ménage, with our cats. Our students were our kids—we never had any of our own. But that was long before Anita got wanderlust. An apt word, I've often thought. She left. Sex was part of it." He paused to light the cigar and blew a wisp of smoke toward the shelves of books. "The scholar's life is a solitary one, don't you think? Right from the monastic days."

He seemed to want to draw me in, to make me party to old sorrows, perhaps, but I wanted to get the talk back to Jerry Corbin.

"When Corbin was your student," I said, "what was the relationship like?"

He frowned. "What are you looking for, Mr. Rasmussen?"

"I don't know. Memories?"

He studied me a moment from under tented eyebrows, then he opened his desk drawer and took out a photograph. He studied that a moment, too, then handed it over. It was a group photo. I wondered why it wasn't on the wall with the others. In it stood a much younger Alfred Westrake flanked by a pretty woman and a tall young man. All three of them were grinning. The young man, without the beef he had now, was Jerry Corbin. He wore his hair in a flattop that gave him the clean-cut looks of a young Johnny Unitas. He stood to the left and slightly behind Westrake and was holding the veed fingers of his right hand above the professor's head. Westrake either was blithely unaware or was enjoying the foolery.

I handed the picture back. "Mister Late-Night Comedy."

"A fellow of infinite jest? I thought so for a time. Hoped so." Westrake was staring at the photo, as if teleporting himself back in time to when it had been taken. Thirty seconds went by. A minute.

"But?" I prompted him.

He glanced up. "Do you know what was meant in Shakespeare's day when a man was horned with that sign?"

I hadn't, until just that moment. My face must have signaled my recognition. He said, "Jerry Corbin was also coming to see my wife—that's her there—though I honestly don't believe any of us knew it at first. Eventually, only *I* was in the dark."

What did you say to a man who's just labeled himself a cuckold? I kept quiet: the way Curtis Smyth had the other night in the boiler room when he had stopped himself from telling me his suspicions. I had an idea now of what Smyth had been about to say.

"I'm a decade older than Anita," Westrake went on. "I met her when I first took the job here. She was a popular teacher, new on the humanities faculty, too. Corbin represented what, youth?"

"How did you find out?"

"I saw them together, coming out of a thicket along the river. They were laughing. They stopped and he picked a willow leaf out of her hair . . . and I knew."

"Did you confront them?"

"I never did." Westrake knit his brows and looked down. He brushed a few shreds of spiral notebook paper and tobacco flakes off the desk. "Maybe I felt I had made Anita's life miserable in other ways. You see, I . . ." He glanced at the books lining the room and sighed. "Like many a person who's good with words, I'm remarkably inept when it comes to voicing my pain. I felt betrayed, angry, hurt, even—in an odd way—lustful. In spite of what students sometimes perceive as a misbegotten old fool, I'm quite human. Are you in a relationship, Mr. Rasmussen?"

"Not anymore."

He smoked philosophically a moment. "What remains is an actor's trunk of missed cues, stage anger, bad lines."

"Where's your former wife now?"

"Wisconsin. She's a grandmother. She laughed over this photograph. She said that of all the students she'd known, Jerry Corbin meant the most, and the least. At any rate, I didn't act on my passion. Not then—not now. If that's what you're asking."

"I guess I was."

"Then you have your answer. All of that was ages ago."

We looked at each other without our eyes quite meeting. He said, "Good night, Mr. Rasmussen."

I stood. All the books, the plays, the high culture, and where had it gotten him? He had checkered himself into a lonely corner. I closed the door as I left.

15

"HOWDY, MR. R.," Gripaldi said when he opened the hotel suite door at 7:40. He was slightly out of breath. "Come in. Mr. C. is with the press."

My hackles went up; I had expected to meet with Corbin alone. "What's wrong?"

"Not a thing. They love him."

Gripaldi had been using a pair of push-up stands when I arrived. Under his yellow tank top, his pectorals glowed. I followed him through the alcove into the main room, where Jerry Corbin stood with half a dozen people I didn't know. There was champagne. Gripaldi punched my arm and went on down the short corridor to one of the other rooms.

"So as a last resort," Corbin was saying, "desperate, the guy goes to this swami, with the headgear and all, and the swami bows and says, 'You've got to cut out some things.' " Corbin was into it, scrunching his body down, doing the swami voice, saying, " 'No liquor, no cigarettes, no greasy foods.' And the guy goes, 'It's that simple?' 'Yes, that simple,' the swami says. The guy goes, 'Well, you're the doc . . . booze and butts, sayonara. But what about women? I mean, you didn't say nothing about giving up women.' And the swami bows and says—"

Corbin saw me and stopped. He straightened. He looked at his guests and held up a finger, signaling that he'd be right back. He came over, asking his question with a jab of his chin.

"Hold the punch line and keep them waiting," I said. "You sly old showman, you."

He didn't smile. "What's up?"

I wondered if Justin Ross had remembered to tell him I was coming. "We gonna talk?" I said.

"You've got something?"

"Maybe."

"Come back in a half hour. I've got these reporters."

"You don't want them digging up what I've got to tell you," I said.

"And what's that?"

"An old story about you and Anita Westrake—for openers."

He frowned. He started to say something, then didn't. He took me by the shoulder. "Wait in the next room."

Two minutes later, he joined me in the room set up with the phones and fax machine. "Where'd you hear that?" he demanded.

"From the guy you put the horns on," I said. I told him what I had learned.

His mouth made a tight line, angry maybe, or just resistant. "I don't like the idea of you rooting around in my past. I hired you to protect me."

"It's useful to know where potential danger lies," I said. "My experience is it tends to come from behind us. It's possible Lowell is your boneyard."

"Where I've got the bodies buried? Bullshit!" He scowled and went into the bedroom. It was as if, having spent his time in that most ephemeral of media, he had lost all sense of the long chains of cause and effect which linked the present with the past. In television, several seasons represented longevity. He appeared in the bedroom doorway with his shirt unbuttoned. "Did Westrake tell you anything else?"

"Like what?" I asked.

He watched me closely a moment, then shook his head. His

intensity softened and he called me into the room while he changed into a fresh shirt that someone had laid out for him on the king-size bed. "Yeah, Anita and I had a thing," he said. "It didn't last long, barely a semester. But it wasn't just adolescent erotica." His right hand went up. "She was the most interesting woman I'd known."

With men it was always possible to cloak actions in the safety screen of goatish lust. I respected that he didn't, even though, for a student, bedding a popular professor had to have been a coup.

"The way it was," Corbin said, "I had become tight with Westrake. I liked listening to him. He knew about all kinds of things that weren't part of my reality. Literature, the theater. He was a pretty hip guy. Hell, he probably still is. Justin says he wears a ponytail. Anyway, I used to go over their place sometimes. Anita would be there, and she'd fix tea. But it wasn't the routine I'd always experienced—you know, leave the menfolks alone to talk. She was an equal. She was a lot younger than him. Nice looking, and nice, too. Bright. The attraction was probably growing, though I wasn't aware of it at first. One night I ran into her in the library. It was the first time we'd been alone together. We . . . connected. It was an early spring night, with forsythia and all."

"And gypsy violins?" I said.

"Ah, Jesus, I don't know why I'm telling you this. You really think it relates?"

"It might." I sat on the foot of the bed.

He began to pace slowly. "I walked her home, and she invited me in. It happens Westrake was away, giving a paper at a conference. I stayed the night—talking; maybe we read some poetry. At dawn we went to bed."

Corbin's voice had softened with the telling, as though the spring night were upon us now. He roamed the hotel bedroom. "We got together a lot after that, in my room, along the river.

Once in her office, on the desk! God, she was hungry for it, all of it. I was just . . . hungry. It was one of those intense, frantic, lovely affairs." He stopped moving. " 'Lovely.' Sonofabitch! Is that stupid?"

"What ended it?"

"Spring ended. I don't know. I met someone . . . someone else."

Corbin went to the mini-bar, opened it with a key, and squinted at the selection before drawing out two dwarf cans of beer. He held one up. I shook my head. He popped open a can and took a pull that must nearly have drained it.

"What about Westrake?" I said. "Wasn't he a friend?"

"You think he's the one sending the notes?"

"Do you?"

"Justin thinks it could be."

"Is Justin aware of what you've just been saying?"

Corbin thought about this and shook his head. "He'd have mentioned it. We bumped Westrake's Shakespeare. Justin thinks envy is motive enough. Simmering frustration."

"Sometimes is," I said. "Though it seems kind of thin after all this time."

"So where are we?"

I rose and went over to the big window, looking past our reflections at the night. The mill buildings on the other side of the river glimmered with lights. What once had been sweatshops were now costly condominiums. I wondered who was in them and what they might be doing. I wasn't impervious to what Corbin had been telling me. In a way I envied him the emotional risks he had taken, the passion he had felt. It made his life bigger than mine in a sense, and diminished my own, and it reminded me in a way I didn't need to be reminded that Lauren was really gone.

"The first night I met Justin," I said, turning, "he told me he's a man who gets things done. I'd guess most of the time he does, but he's been schooled by television. His method is full frontal attack."

"Doesn't always appreciate the situational subtleties, huh?" Corbin said.

"Something like that."

"And are there subtleties here, Rasmussen?"

"I think so."

"What are they?"

"Why don't you tell me?"

Surprise—then anger—altered his features. "What?"

"Come on, Jerry. The love story is touching, but you're wasting your money if you aren't going to give me the rest."

"Shit! Is this the kind of help I'm buying? Is this how you run an investigation? Well you can walk right the hell out that door!"

I said nothing. I kept looking at him. I didn't move.

He went over, grabbed the second beer, and punched it open. He drank. He glared at me and drank some more. He said, "Westrake wanted more than a doting student."

"What?"

"Maybe my affair with Anita was a way of telling him where *my* inclinations lay."

"Wait a sec," I said.

"It's why I put the horns on him in that photograph."

"Are you saying—?"

"He liked guys *and* chicks. Okay, Mr. Detective? He came on to me. Satisfied?"

I nodded slowly. "Okay."

"And forget the outburst. I want you to stay with it. You came recommended."

I remembered Justin Ross saying that the night he'd hired me, but he had never explained. Before I could ask now, the fax machine in the adjoining room beeped and came to life. Corbin and I both watched a sheet of paper curl slowly into the reception tray. He picked it up. As he read it, several emotions came and went on his face.

"Another one?" I said.

He handed the sheet to me and sank into a chair.

The fax had been sent from Los Angeles, from the Starr and Brown Agency, at 5:12 West Coast time.

> *Jer: Just talked to Steelsmith over at network. The shit-heel won't come right out and say it, but they're probably not going to pick up your option after this season. Man, I am truly sorry. But listen: my contact at VARIETY says tomorrow they're running a piece on your new show that will up the salivation factor considerably! Bad news is you're out. Good news is you're in.*

The message was signed with a little star; agent Starr, I assumed. Corbin said listlessly, "I wish it just said, 'I'm going to kill you.' "

I handed back the fax.

"I guess this puts paid to our discussion about why I keep you around, pal," he said. "Now I've *gotta* stay healthy, and out of the bad-news column. The good news is . . . you're in."

"Only if I'm free to do what I have to. Ask my questions where I ask them."

He balled the message and hit the can with it. He pushed to his feet slowly. "What the hell do people expect? They see us on TV, smiling and full of wit, flirting with starlets, and they think that's reality squeezed into that box, that hour. They're sitting in their living room in bunny slippers with a glass of milk, thinking my life is bigger than theirs, for God's sake, that I'm having a ball. It's a crock. Fairy dust and mirrors. It's the scared little man behind the scrim, talking through the megaphone, trying to convince everyone he's the Wizard of Oz. We're ego freaks. We're surrounded by people who kiss our ass but hate us. We drink too much. Our personal relationships are crash sites. My third wife is holding me up for a shitload of money, and I'm paying lawyers and accountants a shitload to keep it from happening. And what's the payoff? We get laid a little more than the average person. And we make a lot of money. You got any idea how much I've made since we started this conversation?"

The question was rhetorical; he was still talking. "What nobody sees is it's all crap. That fax hurts. I'm the same guy now I always was. I'm no different than anyone."

"Your valet still puts your pants on one leg at a time," I said.

His reaction teetered on anger, then tipped over to a cheerless smile. "I envy you, man," he said. "How much are you worth?"

"Since we started this conversation?"

"You're the first person in long memory who's told me to my face to go take a flying leap. That's worth something." He sighed. "Yeah, ask your questions. Do what you're hired to do. I need you, man."

On the subject of need, I told him about his fan, Curtis Smyth, over at the boiler room at the university. I asked if we could get him a complimentary ticket to the show.

"I'll take care of it myself," Corbin said.

As he put on his suit coat, there was a knock at the door. Gripaldi called in that the limo was there to bring Jerry to the evening rehearsal. "Want to take a ride?" he asked me.

I told him I'd catch him there.

I was surprised to see some of the reporters still in the outer room. I guessed the champagne hadn't run out yet. Corbin joined them like he had been gone only a moment. His smile was cunning.

"So the guy says to the swami, he goes, 'You haven't said anything about women. Have I gotta give women up, too?' And the swami says—"

I closed the door behind me.

16

ON THURSDAY MORNING I called police headquarters and asked for Ed St. Onge, but was told he had taken a sick day. "That's rare," I said.

The desk officer laughed. "The sonofabitch has got over a hundred accrued."

I made one stop, then drove over to Centralville.

Pronounced *"Centerville,"* it's a section of the city where French-Canadian families staked out turf in the days when the looms and shuttles were going full tilt and the mills were glad for cheap, honest labor. More than a few families had stayed. Vinyl siding in pastel shades was popular on the close-packed homes, along with side-yard shrines of recycled bathtubs set on end in the ground, sheltering statues of Christ and the Blessed Virgin. And now, with city elections looming near, lawns were pegged with campaign signs. Possessed of neither shrine, sign, nor siding, the St. Onge residence made do as a pale gray asphalt-sided ranch with a detached garage. I parked in front.

I was on my way up the cement walk when I heard sounds coming from the garage. The door was up and St. Onge was inside, his back to me. He was puttering among a clutter of garden tools and cardboard boxes.

"Is it catching?" I said from far enough away not to startle him. He turned slowly, squinting out into the rectangle of daylight at my back. He didn't go for a gun. I went in. "What're you looking for?"

The gray cardigan he wore over a T-shirt exaggerated his shrug. "Purpose," he said. "Inspiration. Some reason to keep on doing it." He frowned and gazed about. "A leaf rake. I know I put it out here last spring. What are you doing?"

I pulled from a paper bag the bottle of George Dickel I had purchased en route. "I was going to wait till Christmas, but it sounds like it might be in order now. Unless the doctor says—"

He took the bottle. He set it on the workbench that ran along one side of the garage, then hunted in a straw picnic hamper and came up with two plastic tumblers printed with watermelon slices. He blew the dust out and poured a couple fingers in each. He didn't ask me if it was too early. Plastic doesn't clink the way glass does. I took a hit and grunted approval. He just drank.

"Remember," I said, "only one of us will be getting a beribboned something under his tree this year. Doesn't have to be big, as long as it's expensive."

We drank. Then I said, "Have you talked to the Murphy woman in the hospital yet?"

He resumed his search, gazing up at the bare pine joists. I looked up, too, at a deep-sea fishing rod, a set of studded snow tires, a dented aluminum thermos cooler and Stein Eriksen's first pair of skis. No leaf rake.

"Any special cause for the high spirits, or is it just autumnal?" I asked.

"You a visiting nurse?"

I sat on a stool at the workbench while he poured two more.

"You should stick to finding bad guys," I said.

His stubbled cheeks puffed out with a sigh. "It's not anything you can see. I don't know. I was analyzing it. Katy phoned, said she's not coming for Thanksgiving, might not even make Christmas. She's on call, this new program she's in."

Katy was Ed and Leona St. Onge's older daughter, a nursing student in Albuquerque.

"But it's not that," he went on, avoiding my eyes. "It's . . . nothing."

"And everything?"

His gaze came up for just a second. "Couple weeks back, when we had that bad weather, we were up at the mall. Leona was in shopping; I stayed in the car. The air was full of sleety rain, and I thought, 'OK, this is it. Winter's coming.' Then this sound starts to come to me, you know, slowly, but building, and finally I realize what it is. I open the door and look up, and moving through the crud there's this long, jagged V of Canada geese. I felt this clean rush of . . . I don't know, *joy*. I got out. I wanted to just feel that with other people, to know we all still share *some*thing. The parking lot's full—they're loading crying kids into safety seats, futzing packages into hatchbacks—but no one's aware. I wanted to shout. There're these birds moving through the murk up there, intent on a purpose, maybe telling us something. And no one's aware."

"Except you," I said.

He tossed back the bourbon. "I'm wondering maybe it's time to take an early out—the pension's still decent—and head for the Sunbelt. Katy says New Mexico is great. I liked golfing the two times I tried it."

"It's something to think about," I said.

"Drink to it," he said and poured more bourbon and we did. I didn't talk. He wasn't looking for a therapist, only a listener. He said, "Yeah, I spoke with the woman who got mugged. She's got some memory loss. Doesn't recall the attack, or why she was there. It may come back. But she brought up a name I'm starting to trip over."

"She and Corbin were classmates," I said.

"And she was on that quiz team as an alternate. She helped drill Corbin and the others. She says she got the idea the coach might've had the questions in advance."

"Professor Westrake?"

"I guess that's the one."

"She thinks it was rigged?"

"It's possible. Mean anything?"

I studied the tread on the snow tires: still good, but studs were forbidden on Massachusetts roads. I met his gaze. "All right, you leveled with me and you're looking for something back. Only I don't know what it is yet. On my side of the street, there's no pension, no golden parachute, which is why I have to keep flapping my arms and not my lips. I did tell Corbin I can't do what you people can. I'll keep working on him to talk to you. That's all I can say right now."

St. Onge's gaze didn't waver. I said, "For the record, I like Canada geese, too. And I hear what they say. If they're heading south already, you better forget about leaf rakes and look for your long johns. You going to be okay?"

"You were."

"Me?"

"After you lost your shield, and when Lauren left. I saw you go pretty deep there, but you bottomed out, and you came back."

"Yeah."

"We manage," he said.

I lifted the plastic tumbler. "A testament to the indomitable human spirit. I say man will 'not merely endure but . . .' " I put the glass down on the workbench. St. Onge stared at me. "I've got someplace I need to be," I said.

The someplace probably wasn't absolutely essential. I pretty much had the gist of what I wanted, but I was relying on years-old memory from a college lit class. I took a spot marked RESERVED FOR BUILDING INSPECTOR near City Hall and went into the public library. On a table I laid out copies of the notes Jerry Corbin had received. The first note, which Justin Ross had brought the night he'd hired me in the Copper Kettle, concluded with the line: *hear the Gong of Doom.* The third note said: *W.F.'s Stockholm address—you won't even hear it.*

The *Viking Portable Faulkner* had the text of the speech, delivered in 1950 when Bill accepted his Nobel prize in Sweden. It wasn't exactly the way I'd scatted it in St. Onge's garage, but close. In it Faulkner said, " . . . when the last ding-dong of doom has clanged and faded from the last worthless rock hanging tideless in the last red and dying evening, . . . even then there will still be one more sound. . . . "

As it had when I'd first read it long ago, the speech sent a shiver along my backbone—but now for a wholly different reason.

17

I TELEPHONED THE alumni office at Harvard from a phone booth in front of City Hall and asked for Judy Bishop. I gave her my name, and she said, "The film-noir guy."

"I'm thinking of a boxing film from the late forties," I said. "*The Set-Up*. Got a star?"

"That's easy. Robert Ryan and Audrey Totter. Ryan was an Ivy Leaguer—did you know that? Dartmouth, class of thirty-one."

"You're good, Ms. Bishop."

"I could show you how good, Alex Rasmussen." She gave her throaty laugh. "How are you?"

"Not quick enough, but still curious. Those four people I asked about before—any of them have kids or grandkids at Harvard now?"

She didn't think the folders had been refiled yet. I held while she checked. No music this time. She came back two minutes later. "One had a daughter who graduated from Radcliffe ten years ago. Another had a son here, but he left last spring before finishing his third year."

The daughter was living and working in China. The kid last spring was a Paul Chapman. Son of Tom Chapman, who had drowned. There was no current address. "Helpful?" she asked.

"I don't know. Do you happen to know if Tom Chapman's body was recovered?"

"Hmm, I don't. I'll see if I can find out."

"One other thing when you get a chance? I'll owe you." I gave her Alfred Westrake's name.

She said she would try. Her office was beginning its fall canvass that evening, telephoning alums to get pledges. "I'll be out straight the next few days, but after that my nights are my own. I noticed that *Laura* is showing next week at the Brattle, on a double bill with *The Dark Corner.*"

"Check that info for me," I said, "and I'll buy the popcorn, too."

I grabbed coffee and a sandwich at Arthur's Diner, then drove over to the university and watched the rehearsal for a while. I thought *my* line of work was routine. Corbin was smooth up there, going through the material time after time, perfecting it with each pass, enjoying himself. But some of the talent needed help; I wished I had a gong handy. At 3:00 the director called a break, and Corbin, accompanied by Chelsea Nash and Phil Gripaldi, disappeared backstage. Justin Ross came over.

"You discovered anything?" he asked. I filled him in up to my visit to the library, leaving out St. Onge. Ross didn't seem impressed with my literary acumen. "It isn't much," he said skeptically.

"You had to be there."

"Are you armed, at least?"

I patted the breast of my jacket. "Eberhard Faber, fine point."

"What?"

"I'm not packing," I said. "I believe in winning hearts and minds."

"Jesus Christ, Rasmussen, this isn't a joke. How can you call yourself a professional and not carry a gun?"

"It's rough. I'm like a surgeon without a pogo stick. When there's someone to point it at, I'll have a gun."

He might have said more, but Jerry Corbin came over so

Ross settled for cinching up his bolo tie. Chelsea came too, clutching her clipboard. She had on a white mohair sweater and black jeans bloused into black cowgirl boots; I hoped she wasn't catching what Ross had. Gripaldi cruised the area, as unobtrusive as a stagecoach. Jerry asked my opinion of the show, and I kept it to a neutral "interesting"; I wasn't being paid as a TV critic. I ran through my list of nonachievements for him. He was more gracious than Ross had been, but he said he didn't see how the quiz bowl had any link with the notes being sent to him. In fact, he was starting to believe that the whole episode with the notes had run its course. There hadn't been a new one for a while.

When the director called everyone back to the set, Corbin said, "Chelsea, honey, it's too nice out to be cooped up in here. Why don't you go back to the hotel and take a swim?"

"I'd prefer to stay," she said.

"You wanted to see Lowell. We're going to be tied up indefinitely. Rasmussen, take her hay riding or pumpkin carving or whatever the hell they do here this time of year."

"Elect cronies to public office," I said and shrugged. "Yeah, it's okay with me."

"Gripaldi will be here. I'm fine. You two go ahead."

Looking less-than-thrilled, Chelsea took her bag and clopped up the auditorium aisle in her boots, with me behind. I snapped my fingers. "You know what would sound great with those?" I said. "Spurs."

We were riding west along the river before Chelsea realized I wasn't headed downtown. She made a brief protest, then sank back. I kept driving. Corbin had been right: it was too beautiful an afternoon to be indoors. The trees were ablaze, and the river was spangled with floating leaves and the reflections of big white clouds. When we were in the Nashoba Valley, a few miles out of the city, I said, "Ever been apple picking?"

"Is this another joke?"

"We've got the best McIntosh apples anywhere. We can get a peck or a half-bushel, maybe split it, Macs and Cortlands."

"Great. And what am I going to do with a sack of apples?"

"Eat them. Have the hotel chef bake a cobbler, or apple crisp. Or there's deep-dish pie, apple spice cake, applesauce."

Chelsea was smiling skeptically now. "Rasmussen's one hundred things to do with apples?"

"Thousand," I said. "Put them in a big tub of water and bob for them on Halloween. Dip them in caramel, hang them on strings. Or throw them at the so-called talent on Jerry's new show."

Her amusement vanished. She didn't waste energy asking if the Bobcat had a car phone. At her insistence, I pulled over to the next booth we came to, at a farm stand in Westford, and she used it. When she came back, I said, "Rehearsal came to a grating halt. There's an all-points bulletin out for you."

"I just wanted to be sure everything's okay."

I couldn't tell whether or not she was disappointed. Emotional camouflage was a skill that the members of the Corbin troupe had down cold. Since we were there, I said, why didn't we check out the farm stand? Her shrug wanted for enthusiasm.

We made our way along aisles of pumpkins, squashes, corn, fresh honey, maple syrup, cranberry products, and apples—lots of them. In back, facing the orchards, there were picnic tables and chairs. I bought two cups of fresh-pressed cider, and we went out.

"Is baby-sitting part of what a P.I. does?" Chelsea asked.

"It's a change from shooting people, which is what Justin seems to want me to do."

"He's just edgy. We all are."

"Not Jerry, apparently."

"He's putting on a brave front for the rest of us."

"One big edgy family," I said.

We sipped cider and watched a tractor pull a hay cart full of small kids past, some of them in costumes. Chelsea said, "When I was about three, I saw a picture of a skeleton in a magazine. My mother explained what it was, and I thought she said the 'skelly man.' The image frightened me for years, so one time my father got me a costume—one of those hokey black pajama things with the painted bones. They thought it would get me over the fear."

"Did it work?"

Her smile was tentative. "Not entirely. Fears grow up, too."

"Are your folks still alive?"

"My father died when I was in high school. Mother died a year ago."

I nodded.

"I was married, too," she said. There was a soft, confessional note in her voice. I looked at her but kept quiet. "His name was Drift. Drift Kirkwood. He was going to be a movie star, and he thought it had the right sound. He sure had the looks. We met at the beach."

"That really happens in California, huh?"

"It did for us. Things started so . . . romantically. Soon though it got pretty clear he was never going to earn a living. He was in love with the *idea* of being an actor, but certainly not the work of the craft. He preferred to lie around the pool at the apartment complex waiting for calls. At night he wanted to be out cruising the clubs. Visibility was the key to being discovered, he used to say. I'd be exhausted from working all day as a production assistant over at Warner. In those days I was full of the idea that I wanted to direct." Another wistful smile. "Still, I'd go, just to be with him. He was that handsome." Then her smile was gone. "He was a drainer, though. He used other people's energy. And, it turned out, a hitter."

"He hit *you?*"

"Not often, only when he felt really pressured."

"Once is too often," I said.

"It's an old story. He'd beg, I'd stay. It was the whole sad, bitter dance of a couple in trouble. I've got scars, mostly emotional. The vision in this eye isn't quite right." It was the eye that tipped outward slightly. "Finally I left. He tracked me down, and when I refused to take him back, he got mean, said he wouldn't let me go . . . not unless I gave him everything. Half, I'd been willing to, but not everything. I'd worked too hard. Plus, my mother got sick then, up in Seattle. So much of my energy had been going into Drift, I'd lost touch with my own mother. Finally I knew that since he wasn't going to let go, I had to find a bar to pry him loose with."

"Is that when you hired the investigators?"

She shut her eyes and nodded. "I didn't like having to. It seemed sneaky. They trailed him around on his night adventures awhile, and they found something I could use."

I entertained a notion of what I'd like to have used on Kirkwood to knock him on his lazy ass. After a moment, Chelsea said, "I confronted him with the proof that I knew. He was smart enough to see that it would ruin his dream of a career, so he backed off. I gave him a few thousand dollars, and that's the last I saw of him. I got the job with Jerry soon after and brought my mother back to Los Angeles for the last months of her life. I've been with Jerry a year and a half now. He's like a father to me, and the work is involving."

I grinned. "That's like saying a tiger shark has a good appetite."

She drank some cider. "Aren't you going to ask what the investigators found out about Drift?"

"Not unless it was sending menacing notes to people."

"You mean to Jerry?" She shook her head. "Drift is incapable of taking that much initiative. Anyway, the last I heard of him, he'd found another pliable little wife." She smiled. "So, what about you?"

"Putting the squeeze on Jerry?"

Her eyes had got some of their sparkle back. "Is there anyone home baking apple cobbler whom you ought to be phoning to say you're doing charity work?"

"Nope. And when there was, we split the cooking fifty-fifty. Her half just tasted better. She's in Florida now, making a new life."

"Do you have her picture?"

"No, but I still know what she looks like. And I know if a chance came to get her back, I'd jump at it. But that's not going to happen."

I kicked the topic around a bit, more than I'd done with anyone in the slow march of time since Lauren had left. Chelsea was a good listener, which made me an okay talker, up to a point. Then it was getting late. The afternoon had faded around us, the air cooling and bringing the smells of harvest and dying leaves. It would be dark when we got back to the city.

While Chelsea used the bathroom at the farm stand, I called my office and punched in the code to access my machine. There was one message. Chelsea came out as I hung up. "I'll drop you at your hotel," I said.

She looked at me. "Was that about Jerry?"

"It might be. I'm going to find out."

If she had hesitated, I might not have agreed; but she didn't. She said, "Take me with you."

18

ON THE RIDE back to Lowell, I told Chelsea about my arrangement with Vito, the historian from Kappa Tau, Jerry's old college fraternity. I omitted the graffiti that claimed Big J had *planked* Betty Crown; it seemed needlessly coarse. Vito's half of the forty bucks was apparently getting lonely. His message on my tape said he had a lead. There was a Betty Crown who used to be a singer, he said, at a place called the Canal Club, but he didn't know where it was, or when. That was okay. He was just a student. He couldn't be expected to know little details about the city's past: like where or what the Canal Club had been all those incarnations ago, before it became Matt's Silver Dollar, and a few other things.

I did.

The building had been run-down when I used to borrow my old man's Falcon and sneak dates inside. SILVERADO LOUNGE it was called now; half the lavender and green neon in the sign had fizzed out long ago. LIVE MUSIC * ALL NUDE REVIEW. But that was its current identity. Back when the hat I wore was standard equipment on men, the Canal Club used to feature some of the best jazz north of Boston.

I pulled into a parking lot full of pickup trucks. Inside the entry, facing us as we went in, was a sign: *Shirts and Shoes Required,* under which someone had written: "Bras and Panties

Optional." Chelsea glanced at me. "I can still take you back to the hotel," I said.

She shook her head.

"Better take my arm, at least."

"I can look out for myself."

"Not you," I said. *"Me.* I don't want to get hit on."

The darkened room was smaller than I remembered it. Of course I was a beardless youth when I sometimes used to go there to watch the bands that blew through Lowell. The art deco was gone, too. The walls were flat black, speckled with sequins, to give the place the look of a silver mine, I guessed. There was a bank of poker machines and a pool table on one side. In back, a partition wall cut off some of the area for an office and restrooms. A sour fog of smoke and perfume circled our heads.

As we started in, a man slid off a high stool and shuffled over. "T'ree dollar cover charge, folks," he said in a voice that squeezed its way through mashed cartilage.

I knew the voice, like I knew the face under the gray scali cap with the little shamrock on it. "Kid," I said to its owner.

He leaned close to study me. "Hey, I didn't rekanize ya."

It wasn't mutual. His face looked like a pie plate that had been run over by a dump truck and banged back into shape by a tin-knocker with the d.t.'s. I was accustomed to seeing him in baggy sweats and work boots, shadowboxing his way along the esplanade when I ran there, calling the rounds in his Andy Devine voice. Old habits die hard.

"I didn't know you worked here, Kid," I said.

"Doorman." He grinned at the euphemism; he could dribble any gate-crasher like a rubber ball.

He looked at Chelsea like maybe he should ask for some ID, but he didn't. I gave him a ten and showed an open hand that said keep the change. "Matty Silver still above ground?" I asked.

"So's the Bunker Hill monument."

"I thought that was you."

He grinned. "Get a table. I'll send a waitress over."

He shuffled off, and Chelsea asked the question with her look. "He won some Golden Gloves titles a lot of rounds back," I said. "He had a pro career under the name Kid Sligo—most of it spent having his face turned to hamburger because he wouldn't go down."

"Is he okay?"

I shrugged. "What's okay? In his ear, the final bell has never rung. He's friendly."

We made our way to a little Formica circle held up by stainless-steel legs. The pickup trucks in the lot weren't for show. The place was busy, mostly with people at the bar which ran parallel to a runway where some women were performing. In the colored spotlights cutting the air it took me a moment to realize the group was a band: a half-dozen women in red-and-black-satin teddies, net stockings, cowgirl boots, and cowgirl hats, playing and singing what might pass for country-and-western music if you'd never heard Patsy Cline. A pair of bartenders in red vests were shagging drinks. They weren't pouring any Fuzzy Navels that I could see.

A waitress appeared, almost as overdressed as the band members. One hand was a banking operation, bills curled over her fingers like green rings. Chelsea declined; I ordered a beer. Five bucks. Good deal. At the end of the runway was a sign, PLEASE DO NOT TOUCH THE PERFORMERS WHEN THEY ARE WORKING. Afterwards was maybe another story.

"What's any of this got to do with Jerry?" Chelsea asked over the noise.

Before I could figure that out, Kid Sligo said close to my ear, "Okay, c'mon wit' me." Even his whisper sounded hoarse.

Matty Silver hadn't changed, except to turn sixty. With his chin lifted slightly, as if listening to things only he heard, he sat behind his desk: shades on, gray goatee, white shirt with blue suspenders. The deck of Chesterfields, one burning in a tin ashtray, spinning smoke up into the cone of light from a desk lamp, lay in ready reach. He was rolling coins on a little pull-out tray meant to support a typewriter. There were posters on the walls, and old playbills, as yellow as March snow around a city hydrant. When Four Roses quit distilling, it was a sad day for this place. Kid Sligo said, "Okay, Mr. Silver. I brung him."

Silver sat in a blue haze. I forgot and gestured with my head to the room beyond the wall, where the music was. "What happened, the costume trunk get hijacked?"

Sligo gave a wheezy laugh. "You don't pay no attention to how bad they play though, right? Sorry, miss."

Silver had not moved. I don't think he had breathed yet. I said, "I'm trying to get some information."

He plucked a dime from a pile and set it with a soft click on the edge of the desk. "There's a booth down the street where it's quiet. Stick it in and dial four-one-one."

I ignored the dime. I could have said something about having done him a favor a few times when I was on the cops and there were people in town who would have liked to have seen him shut down. But he knew that. I said, "I saw Mingus play here once. I had to sneak in. Cedar Walton I remember another time. Dave Brubeck. Jazz is still alive last I checked, but I didn't look here."

I heard Sligo move his feet behind me. Chelsea touched my arm. Silver said, "How's the front gate, Kid?"

The ex-boxer shuffled out. Silver felt for the cigarette in the ashtray and sucked at it, and I saw from Chelsea's look that it was only then that she realized he was blind. "What kind of information?" he asked.

"Conjure with a name that goes back awhile," I said. "Betty Crown."

Chelsea glanced at me and stepped closer to the desk. Silver smoked, puffing it out in small rings that shimmered on the air in front of his dark glasses like ectoplasm. "Sit down," he said.

There were two wooden chairs that probably had more history than most in the city. We took them. Silver said, "We're talking twenty-five years."

"Maybe more," I said.

"She wasn't the sweetheart of Sigma Chi—I'll tell you that."

"What do you mean?" Chelsea asked.

He made a slow production of stubbing out his cigarette. "She was a tough cookie. A townie. But could sing like a young Rosie Clooney. I don't know if she could've gone far with it or not. She flaked."

"Flaked?" Chelsea said.

"Made like a tree. Took a walk. Split."

"You know what became of her?" I asked.

"What became of Jackie Jensen?"

It was a point.

"Was that her real name?" Chelsea asked.

"If it wasn't, I don't know what was." Silver faced me again. "What is this, gas-from-the-past week? I hear Jerry Corbin's back in town."

"Did *he* used to come here?" Maybe it was the screen of smoke, but Chelsea seemed to have gone a little pale.

Silver lit another weed. "Why not? Plenty of the college crowd used to. Buff up their saddle shoes and stick on a tie. In those days there were always cats and kitties, beer, good music. It wasn't El Morocco or the Hi Hat, but we drew some names. Tell her, Rasmussen. Weekends the place swung."

"What about Betty Crown?" I asked.

Silver smoked. "She was a looker. With hair the color of a brass horn."

"How do you know?"

"I'm blind, not stupid. She waitressed days at a lunch counter in Cupples Square, sang here after hours. Probably wasn't nineteen yet. She got good enough so I gave her a steady date, one night a week, three, four sets with a piano player. She filled in between the acts that booked weekends. For her it was a little under-the-table bread, not a living. But I never got the feeling it had to be. She just loved to sing. Ballads, torch songs, a little scat. She couldn't sing the blues, though. She had the range. Maybe she didn't have the pain."

"Or maybe not yet," Chelsea said.

Silver and I both turned toward her, but she said nothing more. I said, "You wouldn't have an old photo?"

"Nope."

"Did Corbin go with her?" I said. I didn't ask if he'd planked her.

Silver's shrug was minimalist, like all of his gestures. "Big J was a handsome kid, quick smile, a mile of malarkey. Chicks liked him."

"Did Betty Crown like him?" Chelsea asked.

Smoke moved, like shifting layers of memory. "Other way around, I'd say. He used to come around to dig her act. Others did, too. Like I said, she looked and sang good. Corbin got to be a regular stage-door Johnny. Crazy sonofagun. I gather he's had his chick troubles over the years. In town trying out a new show, huh? He should. Get a new bag. Leave the late hours to someone young. That stand-in cat they got is where the show's goin'." Silver ventured the first expression that could be construed as merry. "I'm not knocking him; he swung for a lot of years, gave people a good time. Now he's getting the gong. Hey, when a gig ends, you hustle and book the next one."

"Cowgirl striptease?" I said.

He didn't waste a reply. He dragged his Chesterfield a long moment, then said, "I remember the night Jack Teagarden blew here. His horn sounded like it was filtered through midnight and silk stockings. Sure, jazz is big still, but what is it? People sit around in a dinner theater and sip wine, listen politely to music-school kids in tuxedos. Improvisation means it isn't coming from a machine. The sweat and funk've gone out of it. Kerouac used to fall by when he was in town, beat a tabletop or a brandy jug. This joint was happening. But it all started to turn to sand after Charlie Parker died. And Billie, and Trane . . . There's no soul in it anymore. We got trouser rousers posing as musicians, we push light beer . . ."

The tally went on, and we listened awhile. But his was a bluesy valentine to the old days, and the old days were gone. We left him there shaking his head. Kid Sligo opened the outside door for us, cuffing my arm and kissing Chelsea's hand with a touching gallantry. As we drove back to the hotel, windows down to air out, Chelsea said, "Don't you feel sorry for him?"

"Silver? It's a choice," I said. "He could've retired years ago and gone north, south. Wherever. Those coins added up."

"Was he always blind?"

"He used to like saying he'd taken a beating from some of Lucky Luciano's boys—it made a better story than childhood scarlet fever." I glanced over at her. "You seemed pretty intent back there."

"Was I? Just thinking, I guess. Wondering what those days must have been like."

"Let me buy you coffee somewhere, and I'll tell you all about them. Secondhand, of course."

"I have to get back. It's late, and tomorrow's a big day. Last rehearsal before the show."

"And good old Jerry likes to know where his people are at bed check."

She didn't rise to it. She sat looking out at the city night, and I considered confronting her with what Ed St. Onge had told me about the old quiz bowl possibly having been a fix, but something made me wait. My cop training maybe—holding a detail back, as a measure for future truth. At the hotel elevator, she touched my arm. "Thanks for taking me along."

I nodded. "Any time, lady."

As I got back in my car, the sweet smell reminded me I still had the bag of apples. I was about to take them in to leave at the desk when I saw someone whisk out past the doorman and get into a waiting cab. Only his lower half caught the light as he crossed the sidewalk, and only for an instant; but I'd bet that in all of Lowell there wasn't another pair of ostrich-skin boots.

19

THE TAIL JOB wasn't a tough one. The cab flowed through the evening traffic with its dome lighted and a Day-Glo sign across the rear deck touting a brand of smokes I'd never heard of. An octogenarian with cataracts might have had trouble. We went out Merrimack, past the Wannalancit Mills and across some of the old canals.

Once the power lines for the country's first industrial city, the canals had brought the river's energy in to run dozens of mills and prompted Charles Dickens to call Lowell the Venice of America. They were dormant now, the mills and canals (and some would say the local politicians)—national and state park attractions, catch basins for flotsam. The vast buildings housed what industry they could and kept arsonists working, and once or twice a year the city would drain the canals to find bodies. But there was life here, too, whirring away at every level. At times like tonight, a glitter of autumn mist took the moonlight and neon, old cobblestone and brick, and spun fascination.

At University Avenue the cab went across the bridge, across Pawtucket Boulevard, and all at once I felt smart. My heart drummed a little faster. Sure, Ross could have been prowling for ribs and pinto beans, or bound for the college auditorium to make certain everything was set for tomorrow, but my gut told me otherwise. I dawdled several hundred feet back and when the cab stopped and Ross got out, I parked and waited until the cab left.

There were students out, couples walking back from study dates at the library, no doubt, heading over to the union to sip an ice-cream soda through two straws and groove to Pat Boone records on the jukebox. I stayed well behind Ross. And even when he rounded a corner and I didn't see him I didn't fret. I knew where he'd be.

Canterbury Hall was unlocked, the linoleum corridors night-lit and bright as old amber under their half-century of wax. I climbed the stairs. On the third floor, at the far end, I saw Ross in a fan of light as he opened an office door and went in. I got close enough to smell cigar smoke and hear Ross say, "Thanks for waiting," before the door was closed.

I went nearer. There was an open transom window above the door. Ross said, "We need to talk."

Footsteps and a squeaking noise behind me made me turn. A guy in gray coveralls was wheeling a mop bucket my way, carrying a pair of yellow signs. He set up one of his signs. In the office, a reedy voice said, "It's goddamn late. Sit down." Professor Emeritus Alfred Westrake.

"Passing in a term paper," I told the janitor, advancing several steps toward him, not wanting my voice to carry through the open transom.

He gave me a wary eye. "Kind of old for a student, aren't you?"

"You're not the world's youngest custodian," I said.

He shrugged and set up his other yellow sign. "Yeah, well, watch your step."

I tried to figure a way to hang around and eavesdrop, but short of doing chin-ups on the doorjamb, there was none. I left the janitor swinging figure eights with his mop and went back to my car and waited. Ten minutes later Justin Ross came to the street and stood there a moment until a cab appeared and he got in. I followed. The cab parked briefly outside a sub shop, and Ross went in and emerged shortly with a long paper bag. Moët and caviar went only so far. Last stop was the Riverfront Plaza.

Driving back to my apartment, I scripted variations of what might have gone on in Professor Westrake's office. Heated confrontation; sinister conspiracy; sober powwow: ending with "Let me use your phone to call a cab," or "Hold the anchovies." None of them played better than the rest. At home I made a cheese sandwich, which I ate with an apple. Then I sat in the dark with a beer. Moonlight threw patterns on the scabby wallpaper. Somewhere a train hooted forlornly. I thought about the case for a time, then put it to bed.

Sometime after I'd been asleep, the telephone rang. I practiced once to get the frog out of my voice, then picked up and said, "Hello?"

There was a span of silence, then a soft shrill whining, like a faraway siren, and at last a voice—at least, I think it was a voice. I couldn't tell if it belonged to person or an animal: the sound was deep and rhythmic and distorted. Nor could I tell what it said. There were a lot of slow explosive *f* noises . . . *fuh, fuh, fuh* . . . the way an insect might sound if it could speak German at low speed. I sat up. "What?"

A thin, whispery laughter locked my vertebrae in ice.

I reached for the bedside lamp. "Who is it?" I asked, like I expected an answer.

More soft laughter, trailing away to a tiny click.

Shaken, I set the receiver down and took what comfort I could from the small circle of lamplight in my two A.M. apartment. When I finally put out the light, I lay with the strange guttural voice in my mind, replaying sounds I might have heard, anticipating the phone again. But it didn't ring. My mind supplied the effects, though: the sirening, the insect voice—*fuh, fuh, fuh*—and the laughter that made my room a pit of snakes.

20

WHEN I GOT to my office at 8:45 Friday morning, I telephoned the Riverfront Plaza and got Chelsea. Before I could do much more than say good morning, she said, "I got chatty there yesterday. I said some things I really hadn't meant to get into."

"That's okay. I—"

"Just so we're clear. I'm not looking for a confessor, or anything. I'm here for the show."

"Chelsea, all we did was—"

"Two more days, then it's over, and on to the next place. I've got to stay focused." There was a knock in the background, and I heard her call out, "Be right there."

I said, "I want to ask you something. Can we meet?"

"Today's the final rehearsal."

"Pick the time."

"Besides, Jerry is getting the honorary degree this evening. I've got arrangements to make around town today."

"Is Jerry there?" I asked.

"No. Alex, listen, I have to go." And she did.

There had been a thaw between us yesterday afternoon, but it was gone now, refrozen. I had wanted to ask her about Justin Ross's foray to Westrake's office, tell her about the late-night phone call I had received, but that would have to wait. The telephone rang. It was Judy Bishop at the Harvard alumni office.

* * *

I parked the car *near* Harvard Yard. On the leaf-strewn grass, overweight pigeons and squirrels scampered, oblivious to the tread of urban combat boots, Birkenstocks, and moldy sneakers. A gumshoe seemed to make no difference. On the phone Judy Bishop had said that she hadn't found a current address for Paul Chapman, the student who had dropped out last year. However, she had talked with the Harvard campus police and learned that Chapman had gotten into trouble before he left school.

"What kind of trouble?" I asked.

"He was standing out on his balcony shouting obscenities and throwing things."

"I thought that's what college is about."

"Stark naked in the middle of winter?"

"Yeah, hmm."

"I spoke with the tutor at Eliot House, where the kid lived, and he says Chapman was superbright, apparently. A whiz at electronics. Used to fix things for classmates—computers, stereos, so on. His goal was opening his own company. But he lost interest in his studies after his father's death, became antisocial, quit attending class. The tutor said Chapman took most of his belongings when he dropped out, but left a couple boxes in storage. Would taking a look be of any use to you?"

I figured it was worth a ride to Cambridge.

Eliot was one of the undergraduate living quarters; at Harvard, Judy said, they didn't call them "dorms." She was waiting for me with the storage-room key.

"The tutor just told me that before he left school Paul Chapman got his head shaved and spent his time listening to angry music."

"You know anything about his father's accident?" I said.

"Only that he was alone on his sailboat. Turns out he was broke, evidently keeping solvent by moving paper around. The body wasn't found."

Judy unlocked a door under a stairway and found a light switch. We picked our way past footlockers and steamer trunks with prep-school decals on them, back to where some steel shelves had been erected. Chapman's things were in two cardboard boxes with his name printed in marker pen on the outside. There wasn't much. A small tool kit, some course papers—all A's, I noted—computer magazines, books. Judy exhumed a few Polo dress shirts.

I looked through the books. They appeared to be course texts, mostly: electronics, some engineering. Among them I found a small green leather-covered volume that looked quite old. It had a cross design on it in faded gold leaf, the cross tipped at an angle, its equal-length arms split at the ends and curved back.

"It's a moline cross," Judy said. "A heraldic design."

I looked at her. "How'd you know that?"

She shrugged. "One of the perks of my job—I get to take free classes in the extension school."

"In heraldry?"

"We're talking Harvard here."

The print inside was in a language I didn't recognize. It stumped Judy, too. "It looks a little like books my dad had," she said. "He was a Mason. It's different, though."

We looked through the remaining items, then put everything away. We locked the storage room behind us. As I walked Judy back to her office, where she said she was involved with the alumni canvass, she asked, "What would you like to have found?"

I looked at her. "You thinking about a career change?"

"I enjoy what I do, but that was kind of fun. I kept imagining we were the characters in *Out of the Past.*"

"As long as you don't shoot me in the end," I said.

She smiled. "Then 'fess up. What did you hope to find?"

I shrugged. "Dead man's gold? Or a key to the tower room where a princess used her fingernails to scratch out a secret code? Something to tie Paul Chapman to the case I'm on would've been nice."

"So that probably wasn't very helpful, huh?"

"Kid"—I gave it my best Robert Mitchum—"you never know."

21

I ARRIVED AT the Lowell campus at 2:00. I'd been spending so much time at colleges lately, I could probably make the dean's list. In the auditorium, carpenters, electricians and painters were doing their thing, getting the stage ready for tomorrow night. The guest panelists were up there too and included a former Red Sox player—though not Jackie Jensen—and a small, wire-haired woman who several years before had been on a sitcom I couldn't remember the name of. I couldn't remember *her* name, either. I did recall having seen her more recently in a commercial, slipping doggie snacks to a drooling Gordon setter. Maybe the *New Gong Show* represented a step in the climb back, but with lines like she'd been given, she'd be better off with a pair of basset hounds for straight men.

There was no sign of Chelsea. Morrie the accountant and Phil Gripaldi sat off to one side, playing cards. Morrie's face was screwed up in concentration as he studied his hand. Over on the little desk where he generally sat there was a paper coffee cup and a doughnut box. I hadn't eaten. I opened the box but found only the stale husk of a corn muffin and a lot of cigarette butts. Crinkled among them were a couple of paper streamers. Calculator tapes, I realized. Morrie and Gripaldi were intent on their game, so I took one of the tapes out and pulled it open. Predictably, it was strings of numbers, but next to various items

I saw that someone, presumably Morrie, had written words—abbreviations, actually. The bottom was a debit. The other strip had more of the same. I wasn't sure what they meant, but I put them in my pocket.

When the rehearsal ended, Corbin asked me to drive him back to the hotel. He seemed preoccupied and said little in the car. When we got to his suite, he called room service and ordered a bottle of champagne. "Not impressed with the show, are you?" he said to me.

"How do you like my marksmanship?" I said.

He scowled. "Okay, TV isn't your thing. You're no kind of judge. I am. The show isn't much—I admit it." He sighed. "Maybe I should just hang it up, go out gracefully."

"But?" I said.

He looked at me.

"I've watched you. When you're up there under the lights, you're different. Forget the crappy lines, the bottom-of-the-barrel jokes. You become as close to happy as I've seen you get."

He eyed me with an expression I couldn't read. "It's not just for myself I do it," he said. "It's for my people, too."

"Whatever."

"No, I mean it. They depend on what I do. Chelsea's like the child I never had. And Justin and Morrie . . . hell, I'm thinking of offering Gripaldi a full-time gig. There could be room on the team for a certain private eye," he said.

"Gosh, would I get an ostrich-hide wallet for my license?"

Anger flickered on his face a moment, then was gone. He went into the bathroom. I wandered over to a window and looked out. On the ledge of a building across the canal I could see pigeons, the same soft gray as the old stone lintels, strutting and cooing in the mild sun. They could have been retirees on a bench in Sarasota for all they seemed to care that winter was seven short weeks away. A bellhop brought the champagne and set it in ice. Corbin called out from the bathroom for me to pop it. He came in wiping makeup from his face with a towel, swallowed a quick glass and poured another.

We drank champagne. He drained a third glass and began to wander about the suite, looking at the furnishings and decor as if noticing them for the first time and not finding much of interest there. If his new show worked, he was going to be seeing a lot of hotel rooms. When he spoke, his voice was softer than usual, his words slower. "Some nights you lie awake in the wee small hours, and the mind monkey gets climbing. The questions start. What's it all mean? How long before the prostate blows? Can I ever afford to retire? Like that. Will anyone remember me when I'm gone? And that little drum in your chest going, 'I want . . . I want . . . ' " He looked at me. "Am I full of shit, or does any of that make sense?"

I shrugged. "I've hitched that highway a few times."

He poured more champagne. "You figured out who's sending the notes yet?"

"No."

"Justin's convinced it's Westrake."

"He still think Westrake's angry at being upstaged?"

"I guess so."

"Is that why Justin went on his little mission over there last night?"

I said it casually. Either Corbin was truly surprised, or he was a very good actor. I told him about following Ross to the university, but ending up missing the conversation between him and Westrake. Corbin said he had gone to bed early last night; he knew nothing of the trip, but he hadn't had a chance to talk with Justin yet today. He was sure Justin would tell him. He speculated that Ross was acting on his instincts, telling Westrake to butt out. I wasn't wild with the thought that Ross's instincts might be truer than my own, but I accepted the explanation for now; it made a kind of sense. Like the others on Corbin's team, Ross was fiercely loyal.

"Let's talk about you, then," I said.

"What about me?"

"You got stock in Moët and Chandon?"

Corbin stepped forward so abruptly that champagne sloshed over his hand. He ignored it and drew his bulk into a pose of threat. "What'd you say?"

We were close enough so I could see the artery throbbing in his neck, the fine sheen of sweat on his lip above the capped teeth.

"I could deck you, you know that?" he growled. "I could put you through that goddamn wall!"

"And I could do stand-up comedy on network TV. Come on, Jerry, let's each stick with what we're good at."

He held the pose a few seconds. Then he sighed and his shoulders sank. He retreated.

"Forget the booze," I said. "Let's talk about the money."

"The money," he said tonelessly. "You want more?"

"You go around playing Mr. Beverly Hills, but little indicators say you're in the red, or pretty close to it."

"Dammit, I warned you about probing my personal affairs. How would you like it if I went digging into *your* finances."

"You discover any, I'll give you a finder's fee. Okay, maybe your money situation's shaky, yet you toss it around like a third-term Democrat. You pay me ten days up front when a flat retainer would've done."

"I thought I was buying loyalty."

"For a handshake you would've got confidentiality, which is more practical."

"I was buying that, too. How do you think I found you?"

I thought back to the night Ross hired me. He said he'd been asking around, tracking me all day. Had he got a referral from the Crime Busters Hall of Fame? "I don't know," I said.

"Is the name Devlin known to you?"

"The Belvidere Devlins?"

"I know Basil," Corbin said. "Some juice, huh?"

The Devlins had been in the juice business around town for generations, guiding hands in industry, politics, and business. Basil was the last of the breed; patron of this, benefactor of that, trustee to most everything, though less visibly in recent years. He had to be eighty by now, and probably worth half a million for each of those years.

"Dev and I go way back," Corbin went on. "My parents worked for him and his family. We keep in touch. He arranged for these rooms, got the phones and fax installed. Your name apparently got some press a few years ago, Basil told me, but you've also earned a reputation for keeping your counsel. Discretion's hard to come by these days. There's always some traitor willing to flap his lips to the media."

"The friend who asks not to be identified," I said.

"That's the sonofabitch."

"My discretion also means you can pay me and then bury my report," I pointed out. "Nothing says you've got to talk to anyone else."

"I admit it," Corbin said.

"Wouldn't be the first time someone has. I've got more paper sitting in the bottoms of drawers than a college poet. But what I think doesn't matter a sneeze in a snowstorm. I'm paid for what I *do*. If that's not acceptable, you're the one who says so."

There was a knock on the outer door. Corbin looked at me, and I went over and opened the door a crack. It was a hotel valet with a black academic robe and mortarboard in dry cleaners plastic. I gave it a rustle. Expecting what? For a bomb to fall out? I took it inside. "Dr. Corbin, I presume?"

He ignored it. "Rasmussen, in your trade you've got certain . . . rules, haven't you?"

I hung the robe on a clothes rack. "They're mostly unwritten," I said.

"In my trade, that's true, too. The show must go on. Give

them more than they paid for. And never *ever* let them see you sweat." He paused, then exhaled. "My contract runs out the end of the year. Nothing's been announced formally, but the inside betting is my guest host is going to get my chair on *Good Night* next season. The producers want a change."

Welcome to the land of the little people, I thought. My contracts went day to day. "They consult you?"

"They don't have to. The network owns my contract. I practically had to kiss their ass to get a shot at this new show. Why the hell you think I'm in Lowell?"

"Hometown pride?"

He made a sour face. "I'm here because this is the market I've got to score in. Lunch-bucket cities. The Jell-O wrestling and Candlepins for Cash set. No offense. I've got to start from zero and build an audience, like some goddamn cheese ball." He picked up a bottle and upended it over his glass, letting the last of the champagne drizzle in. "You're right. I *am* walking a thin line. It's still black, but not by much, not for long. How'd you find out?"

Why get Morrie in trouble for being careless with calculator tape? I said, "I'm a highly trained sleuth."

He didn't seem to notice. "Another few weeks," he said. "After that, I won't be worrying about them seeing me sweat. Yeah, the new show has all the looks of a turd. If it sinks, I'll be stumbling, falling down, peeing my pants. I'll be a zoid. An old man, with a laundry bag full of snotty hankies and no one to talk to but myself. You know Sally Reed?"

"Who?"

"Woman on my show today. Former sitcom actress."

"Ah, *that* Sally Reed."

"Know how she pays the bills these days? Hawking dog food and those ridiculous lounger chairs on cable TV. I'll be out of the business, gone, forgotten. And by God, Rasmussen, I'm scared."

His face had a splotchy pallor, and his shoulders drooped; but I couldn't be sure he wasn't acting, or just a melodramatic drunk. This show-biz crowd was getting to me. Still, in spite of it all, I found myself drawn to him. Maybe it was the personal force he could exude when he was on, or that in his own anesthetized way, he was in pain. Maybe I just liked him because he seemed to like me.

"What would a couple grand buy?" I asked.

He laughed. "Serious? God, not much. What're you talking? Your retainer?"

"Call it a loan."

"Well . . ." He rubbed his chin. "It'd keep ex number three off my ass about a week. Or buy us all some more bubbly."

"Deal with the ex first," I said.

His smile went most of the way across. "Rasmussen, you're a prince, you know it? A goddamn prince."

I managed a little tap step on the carpet. "There's no business like show business," I sang.

22

"DOES THIS MEAN I can prescribe for my own hemorrhoids?"

So went Jerry Corbin's opening shot upon being conferred with an honorary doctor's degree. The jokes didn't get much better, but nobody seemed to notice. The assemblage on stage, sitting in their black robes, beamed like a coven of happy witches, and the audience roared. Corbin's speech was classic Mr. Good Night stand-up, with shots fired in all directions, several of the choicest aimed at Harvard and the Ivy League. Amid the laughter, Gripaldi and I drifted around the darkened hall on informal patrol.

"It's his timing," Gripaldi confided admiringly. "Man's got that elegant, offhand effortlessness."

"And he makes it look easy, too," I said.

Chelsea sat with Justin Ross and Morrie. I didn't see Professor Westrake. When the affair broke up, there was a reception line. Then we got the in-crowd herded into limos which took them to the Speare House for dinner. The mayor and half of City Hall hogged Corbin's table, so I slipped out after the salad course to use a lobby pay phone.

"Thank you for calling," sang the voice that answered. "This is Ms. Bishop speaking. How may I help you?"

"It's Rasmussen," I said, never without a glib opener.

"Thank God." Her voice dropped a weary octave. "I've had a hundred people say *no* to me today. Twenty hung up in my ear, a dozen called me names, and one elderly gent, class of 1919, told me to perform an act Candy Samples couldn't do."

"And the alumni canvass?"

"Funny. Pretty dire, actually. We've had only fifteen in pledges all afternoon."

"Fifteen grand's not bad."

"Million," she said.

I whistled. "You weren't panhandling at my old school."

"No? What college was that?"

"You've seen it on matchbooks." I took my pen out of my pocket. "Listen, hi."

"Hi." She laughed.

"Have you had a chance to—"

"Alfred Westrake. I did. He never went to school here."

"Well, it was a long shot," I said, putting my pen back.

"Not so fast. If it's the same person, there was an Alfred Westrake at Harvard in the early 1950s."

"I thought you just said—"

"Not a student, he was an *instructor.*"

I mulled that a moment, then asked, "What field?"

"Elizabethan dramatic literature."

I asked if she knew anything more, like why he had left or where he had gone, but she didn't. She did say that she had mentioned the green book with the moline cross on the cover and odd writing in it to a few colleagues, but no one had any idea what it was. I thanked her for her efforts. We chatted about old movies for a few minutes, and then she had to go. "Quota to make," she said. "Bart Stahl, class of '67, is breathing down my neck."

"Sixty-seven," I said. "Wasn't that the Summer of Love?"

I dug more change from my pocket. In the directory I found the number for the Lowell campus and called and asked for the theater department. When someone finally answered, I asked to be connected with Professor Westrake's office. There was no answer. I got back inside in time to find Morrie polishing off my dessert.

23

THE DINNER PARTY broke up early. Tomorrow night the city would turn out for the launch of *The New Gong Show,* and I had to admit, Lowell was going a little loony with excitement. Local talk shows were doing ticket giveaways, and banners had been slung across downtown streets to announce the event, which would be carried live at 8:00 P.M. At the hotel, as if determined not to be alone with me, Chelsea kept herself surrounded with members of the crew, her clipboard ever in hand. Gripaldi and I coordinated plans for tomorrow, agreeing to meet at the hotel at noon. I got back to my apartment feeling a little ragged.

I hadn't run for more days than I liked. I got as far as putting on my running shoes, but I didn't have the will tonight. I didn't have the makings for a good drink, either, which irked me, so I determined to walk to the liquor store in the shopping plaza, about a mile away. It was a nice mild night. I liked the logic of taking a constitutional to get a bottle of booze; it spoke of a balanced life.

In front of the supermarket in the plaza there was a display of pumpkins, and on an impulse I bought one for the office. Why not? Rasmussen gets festive. Carrying it by its stem, a fifth of Gilbey's in the other hand, I set off for home, whistling. It was just about 10:00 P.M., closing time. The plaza was mostly deserted already, the sodium lamps flaring in the mist like vaporous moons, throwing weak light on the asphalt. To my left, at one end of the big parking lot, a teenager in an orange vest was retrieving shopping carts. At the other end, their diesels purring companionably, several eighteen-wheelers were hunkered down for the night. The autumn moon was near the full.

I was halfway across the lot when I heard a yelp of rubber. Turning, I saw a car. It was two hundred yards away, lights off, moving fast. The driver hit second, and the car swerved with the torque. A little puff of smoke went up from the tires. In that instant of quickening heart, I knew it was coming at me.

There were no curbs or parked cars near, only a lone shopping cart, and beyond that a light stanchion a hundred feet to my left, with its lonely oasis of light. I dropped the pumpkin. I set off with the bottle in its brown paper bag tucked under my arm, like Steve Grogan on a bootleg.

I was running well, but I was no kid anymore, as everyone kept reminding me. Even with adrenaline, I'd lost steps. When I heard the pumpkin pop under fat tires, I knew I was next. The car was almost there, its motor roaring with all the fury of Detroit scorned. I wasn't thinking, just reacting. I faked left, then cut hard in my sneakers, grabbed the shopping cart, drew it to me, and shoved. Its action threw me backward, the cart forward.

The car came in low, a pale sleek speckled shape that never slowed. It hit the stainless-steel cart as I was rolling away and launched it over the windshield and roof. I heard music—just a muffled snatch of weird noise as the car passed—then the mangled shopping cart crashed to the pavement a yard from where I was sprawled, bounced, and clipped my right foot. I rolled and came up in pain.

Tires screaming, the car swung in a big smoking el toro turn and came snorting back, the driver working up through the tranny hard and fast and none too skillfully. Metal grated. The light stanchion was thirty feet away, but my run was no more than a hobble now, my right foot afire with pain.

The car was too near. I lurched to a stop and spun around, bracing for a sidewise dive. Panic pushed an idea into my head. I yanked the Gilbey's out of the sack, drew it back like a dinner bell, and threw.

I saw the driver's arm go up instinctively as the bottle hit the windshield dead center and exploded.

He locked the brakes, sending the car into skid, burning more rubber as he tried to recover. The motor stalled.

I shouted and started toward him in a crippled run. He got the mill going, gunning it till blue smoke poured out, then screeched off. I tried to read the plate in the flicker as it passed under lights, but I couldn't get it all. I heard the weird music again though, and got a glimpse of the person at the wheel.

I'd know him anywhere.

It was the Skelly Man.

I stood in the returning silence, amid the fumes of gin and burnt fluorocarbons, repeating to myself the numbers and letters I'd seen, feeling my heart pound, and aware of something else . . . an image I couldn't quite get my mind around. At the sound of footsteps, I turned. A man about fifty, in work clothes and a Mack Trucks cap, came hustling over, followed by a woman driving an Escort, and the supermarket kid in the orange vest.

"God almighty!" the trucker said. "You all right?"

"Yeah," I said.

"Crazy damn sonofabitch. That pumpkin coulda been your head."

"Yeah."

"About the time he missed you his first pass, I was on the CB to the smokies. Any luck, they'll nail him."

"Yeah," I said. Adrenaline makes me witty.

The kid in the vest pointed. "It was a Camaro, if that's any help. I seen it when he turned."

"Halloween used to be a fun time," the woman said from the

open window of her Escort. "But there's no treats anymore. It's all tricks now."

"Crazy damn driver," said the trucker.

They hung around getting into it—no respect for authority, gangs in the street, too much sex on TV—commiserating. I tried to retrieve the phantom thought that had passed through my head, but the more you try, the less you get. A cruiser did show up. The officer was a young woman with an orange tint to her dark hair, which was short and combed in a ducktail. She was maybe twenty-three, five-four in her thick-soled boots, so the big rubber-gripped 9mm on her belt was out of scale; but she looked like she knew what she was about. Her name tag said she was Officer Aquilina. Some cops would have stayed in the cozy car, licking the point of a pencil and filling out paper, but this one was restless. She wanted to do what she had put the badge on to do. She asked her questions with swift efficiency.

"I can call in the routine if it'll save time," I told her. "I'm friends with Ed St. Onge." Hyperbole has its uses.

"You don't mind?" she asked. "I'd like to see what I can find."

I'd given her the car make and what I had seen of the plate. There was disagreement about the color; the mist and sodium lights were deceptive. The supermarket kid said it had gone up on Route 495 heading south. The cruiser took off in a swirl of dry leaves, no siren or party lights.

The gathering broke up. The kid went to punch out, and the trucker headed back to his rig. The woman in the Escort rolled up her window and drove off. The pain in my foot was easing. I walked home on shaky legs.

All tricks, the woman in the Escort had said. A Halloween prank. My gut told me otherwise.

"Who says cops are never there when you need them?" I said to Ed St. Onge when he answered his phone at police headquarters.

"I do," he growled. "What?"

I filled him in, including a good word for the young cop in the cruiser. The moment of silence wasn't in my honor. "Got a motive?"

"Someone doesn't like me," I said.

"Too common."

"I need an owner. Late-model Camaro, Massachusetts plate 348, first two letters either PK or PR."

"The registry's closed. Check me tomorrow afternoon."

"I need it now."

"Because someone in a fright mask broke your pumpkin? Some detective. You home?"

He called back ten minutes later. 348 PRG. Yellow 1991 IROC Camaro. It had been stolen five days ago from a parking lot in Cambridge. I thanked him.

And then my memory netted what it had been after. Pale yellow with primer spots. I had parked behind the same car over at the university four days ago, the morning someone had tried to strangle Florence Murphy, née Flo Ryan, old classmate of Jerry Corbin and student of Alfred Westrake, found by Chelsea Nash.

I wished I hadn't broken the bottle of gin, though taken all in all, it was a fair loss. I wouldn't have had any ice for a drink, anyhow; it was all in a pan, with my foot in it, and I sat there in the kitchen thinking about things in no special order. Westrake had been a professor at Harvard before coming to Lowell. He would have been what, in his mid-thirties then? So why, on the strength of having been at Harvard, hadn't he gone on to a big university, or a plummy little rich-kid college tucked into the Berkshires? Why a state school whose best chops were in science and engineering? As an academic career move, it didn't make sense. Unless . . . what? Unless something had gone bad. Maybe he hadn't published enough minutiae in obscure scholarly journals and had missed tenure. Still, would that have ruled him out elsewhere? I didn't think so—not after Harvard.

No, it would have to have been something else. But what? Had he planked the dean's daughter—or propositioned his son? Been caught pilfering from the Needy Professors' Home fund? Maybe he'd danced naked on his balcony in January, or murdered someone. I had no answers, only the residual tiredness of the day and a sore foot.

I hadn't been in bed five minutes when there was a knock on my door. I opened it to Chelsea Nash standing there in her leather coat and jeans, the dim hallway light spilling off her glasses. I backed up to let her in.

She glanced around my apartment, distracted. "I took a chance driving over here," she said.

"Well, it's cheap but it's cozy," I said. I reached toward a table lamp, but she stayed my arm.

"I meant driving like this," she said. She opened the coat and shrugged it off.

My eyes hadn't lost any steps. She had no blouse or bra on underneath. Her breasts hung full and free. When I got my breath, I started to speak, but she burrowed against me. I held her, full of questions, my nostrils awake with the spicy night-scent of her and the faint smell of cigarette smoke in her hair. Then her mouth was on mine, and she was pulling at my pajama top.

My hundred questions became one question, which I promptly forgot.

We managed the ten feet to my bed, the path marked with my pajamas and her shoes and jeans and underpants. I don't know where her glasses ended up. The schoolgirl look was surface. Her body was grown woman, superheated now and shining in the bars of moonlight through the blinds. She was all hunger and need, kindling the same in me as she moved against me with frantic insistence. We clung, twisted free, clung again, shifting on the bed like wrestlers in a tiny ring. And finally, when I gripped her, wanting to slow us down, to find some small clear space in my head, she broke free, arching back, eyes closed, and drove her hips against me until there was no chance for anything else and I just held on as she gave vent to one long, emptying cry.

The telephone ringing dragged me from a doze. I rolled to a sitting position and sent a groggy look at the bedside clock. After 1:00 A.M.

There is a sleep mechanism set up in the system: keep the male there after mating to increase chances of forming a bond, building a family, ensuring the future of the race. But what about keeping the female there? The other side of my bed was empty. Chelsea and her clothes were gone.

I picked up the phone and croaked into it. It took me a moment to identify the voice over the twang of guitars, but it was a voice you didn't mistake. "The man wants to see you," it said.

24

THE NEON SIGN at the Silverado Lounge was dead. What I could see of the parking lot as I drew in front and stopped was empty. The main entrance was locked. Some time in the past few hours light rain had fallen, making the pavement shine, but the clouds had gone and a nearly full moon was melting on the horizon. Favoring my sore foot, I walked around to the side door and found it open. I went in.

Except for the exit signs over the doors and the LEDs on equipment behind the bar, the place was dark. The air hung with the stale aromas of tobacco smoke and sweat. There was no sign of Kid Sligo, who had telephoned me. I heard no shuffling footsteps. Somewhere, music was playing softly. It wasn't country rock, it was jazz piano; Erroll Garner, if I was guessing. It was coming from behind the partition wall beyond the bar.

I went around the wall to the office, whose door was open, and looked in. A cigarette tip glowed in the dark. "From the way you're moving, I'd guess you're limping, or Kid put out the light," Matty Silver said from behind the cigarette.

"Both," I said.

"Rasmussen?"

"Yeah."

"Switch by the door."

I'd been in the dark too much tonight; I flipped the switch. A desk lamp came on. Silver was at the desk. The music was a tape, playing on a cassette recorder nearby. With slow, sure motions, Silver laid his hands on an empty glass and a bottle of Seagram's 7 and poured some and pushed the glass across the desktop. He had a glass of his own. "In the old days, the last set would just be starting," he said. "Sit down."

Three hours ago, I was in the mood for this; not now. I felt empty, bewildered and depressed. The smoke—and having been wakened twice—was making my eyes gritty. Silver said, "There's a photo there. See it?"

I picked it up and found myself looking at a young woman. The picture was matted in a pewter frame with an art deco look.

"Describe her," Silver said.

I angled the picture in the lamplight. It was black-and-white, less a portrait than a candid shot, never mind the fancy frame. "She's maybe eighteen," I said, "dark eyes and hair that could be auburn, pulled back, high cheekbones. Pretty." I looked at him.

"Go on."

"She's wearing a pale blouse and a jacket with padded shoulders, a strand of pearls. Behind her there's a man who's older, nice-looking suit, hat shading his eyes." He reminded me of someone. From the movies? Nothing more in the picture was in focus.

"Keep looking," Silver said.

I went back to the young woman. Had I said she was wearing a corsage? I did now. "I'm going to guess this is the 1950s, maybe a little after. So who is she?"

"You've got a daytime job, right?" Silver said. "Besides playing gumshoe?"

"Look, you'll forgive me—I've had a weird night. Normal people are home asleep at this hour."

"Where they belong. We're here."

I let that one go.

"Who she is," Silver went on, "is Betty Crown."

That woke me fully. I looked at her again. If it's possible to like someone solely on the basis of a photograph, I did. She had a vague familiarity, too, like the older man in the suit and hat had. "Where'd you dig it up?"

"Your friend brought it when she fell by."

"Tonight?"

"Few hours ago."

Chelsea? It would have had to have been before she came to my apartment. She hadn't mentioned being here—or having the photograph. My memory brought back the faint tobacco-smoke scent in her hair. "She knew who it was?"

"I don't think she was sure. Once she described it, *I* knew. *I* told her."

"So why did you need me? Why now?" More than just exhausted, I was angry. I'd been left out of things. Not just once, repeatedly.

Silver screwed his cigarette into the ashtray. I could identify with the butt. He said, "I had an earlier visitor today. A blast from the past."

"Who would that be? Betty Crown?"

He picked up his lighter and sparked another Chesterfield. "He was *asking* me about Betty Crown."

That startled me. "Jerry Corbin? Asking what?"

"This squares us, right?" Silver said. "For long ago?"

I looked at him. His dark glasses spilled lamplight and I felt the dead eyes facing me behind them. Old accounts had to be balanced. "Square," I said.

"Corbin asked if I'd ever seen her again. Since the old days. Was she still around? Still singing? I told him she'd disappeared a long time ago. Did I remember exactly when? Had she been married? Stuff like that. Oh, yeah, and was she pregnant when she left? Like I'm supposed to remember from thirty-odd years ago."

“Did you?”

“Yeah,” he said. “Nineteen sixty-two. And yeah again. She was pregs.”

With piano music playing softly, I looked at the photo once more. This time I knew why the young woman seemed familiar, but I didn’t speak. It would have sounded crazy to say I had just been in bed with her.

25

I WOKE IN daylight and for an instant I thought I had overslept, but no, it was early, barely 7:00 A.M. I thought about Chelsea having been there in my bed. And then, while I slept, she had gone. My foot was stiff, my body ached, and what had seemed like satiety last night had left me with jangled nerves. I felt an emptiness and—with thoughts of my visit to the Silverado Lounge—a growing fear. As I got out of bed it came to me: today was Halloween.

A shower and a jolt of strong coffee took some of the sand out of my head, but I was looking over my shoulder this morning, checking the rearview as I drove downtown, standing with my back wedged into the corner of the elevator while I rode to the top floor of the Riverfront Plaza. Beginning with that weird phone call two nights ago, things had started to turn. In the flurry of events leading to my conversation with Matty Silver, I had forgotten about the skeleton driver in the parking lot. It came back to me now. I tried to erase an image of a shattered pumpkin.

I knocked on the door of Chelsea's room. There was a long moment before the door opened. She stared out at me. "Alex."

She was in a white terry robe, and her hair was wet. Hanging behind her on a chair was her blue tank suit. "What is it?" she asked.

"That's what we're going to find out," I said. "Get dressed. I'll meet you in the lobby."

Ten minutes later, we sat amid ferns and busy waitresses in the hotel restaurant, steaming coffee before us. Neither of us had wanted food, nor small talk. I said, "Somebody tried to kill me last night."

Her hand came to her mouth. "Oh, no. After . . . ?"

"Before. I didn't get a minute to tell you."

"Oh, my God!"

"Save the dramatics. I take the pay, I have to expect to deal with the rough stuff. Only I don't like it when the people I'm working for hold out on me. That hand-to-God stuff is a bad joke. All of you—Corbin, Ross—I've got questions about Ross—and *you,* sweetheart. You know things you aren't telling me. It's time for the truth. If not, I go to the cops."

"The police? Why?"

"They might be interested in this," I said. "For starters." I took the pewter-framed photograph from the side pocket of my jacket and stood it upright on the table.

She drew a sharp breath and grabbed for it. I blocked her hand. She struggled for a moment, then withdrew her hand. She threshed it through her still-damp hair. The look she gave me was stricken. In a very soft voice, she said, "Okay. I was going to see you today, anyway. I decided it yesterday, maybe even the day before, but I wasn't ready yet."

"Not ready to talk, anyway."

She lowered her eyes. "This has been going around in my head, driving me crazy. I swam thirty laps, hard, this morning, hoping it would go away. When we went to that noisy bar the other night, the Silverado—"

"Bras and panties optional," I said.

There was pain in her expression. "I was interested in that singer, Betty Crown. It wasn't idle curiosity. There's something I came to Lowell to find out, because it's been . . . haunting me.

I spent most of yesterday running around trying to get answers. And now that I think I've found some, I don't have a clue about what to do. So last night, when I came to your apartment . . ." She exhaled softly, and I saw a tear fall on the place mat. She said, "I'm sorry."

I was, too, I guess. I put a napkin in her hand. In a gentler voice, I said, "A person likes to think he's more than just another kind of exercise."

She nodded.

When she had used the napkin, I said, "Why don't you tell me about yesterday?"

She turned the framed photograph so we could both see it. "I brought this to Mr. Silver and described it for him. I watched his face. He knew. He said this was Betty Crown."

"Where did you get the picture?" I asked.

"I've had it a long time. That day in your office—you asked me who Isabelle Martin was?"

I remembered. I told her now that I had found the name when I'd snooped in the Jer-Cor check ledger. She didn't get upset. She said, "This is Isabelle Martin *and* Betty Crown. She was my mother."

I didn't interrupt with questions; not then, nor after, as she told me that a year before, when it was certain that her mother was dying, she told Chelsea that she had once thought about pursuing a career as a singer. Her mother had moved to California, married Ted Nash, and then Chelsea had been born. Her mother gave up the career idea. "Ted was a good father. He was a draftsman at an aircraft plant, steady and hardworking. When I was in high school, he got lung cancer, from the aluminum dust he'd breathed all those years at the plant. He lived long enough to see me graduate."

Chelsea spent the last year of her mother's life nursing the dying woman, and it was then that her mother told her about her early singing days. "Betty Crown was just a name she picked. Martin was pretty common here in Lowell, where she was born."

"And where she knew Jerry Corbin," I said.

Chelsea nodded. "She didn't say so. After my divorce, after I left Warner Brothers, she suggested I go see Jerry—said she'd clipped a want ad. I got the job. And when my mother died, even though I'd only known Jerry a short time, he sent a generous donation to a charity in her name. I took it to be the kind of thing he did. Then, recently, he covered $10,000 in expenses for her estate. When I thanked him, he mentioned that he'd come from Lowell, too. In fact, he said, he'd once known my mother."

"When she was singing at the Canal Club," I said. "And he was in love with her."

She looked at the photograph. "I know that now. I suspect that's how I got the job with Jerry. My mother must have contacted him."

"This guy in the picture isn't Jerry, though."

"I don't know who it is. There are a lot of questions I don't have answers to."

"Which is why you went over to the university alumni office that first day, isn't it?" I said. "To talk to Florence Murphy."

"How did you know that?"

"I didn't until just now."

She nodded, relieved maybe. "I knew Mrs. Murphy had known Jerry long ago. They'd stayed in touch with holiday cards. I called her as soon as I got here. She told me she had something to speak to me about, too. We made plans to meet Monday morning. Then she was attacked."

"Do you know what she wanted to tell you?"

"No."

Sunlight threw bright shapes on the restaurant carpet. A waitress refilled our cups. "Something began to bother me after you took me to the Silverado," Chelsea went on. "Yesterday I called Los Angeles County Records. Ted Nash was in the army overseas until after I was born. I was eight months old before he and Mom even met."

And suddenly I saw it: as I'd seen it without being fully aware last night, when Matty Silver first showed me the photograph. There was a similarity of coloring, something in the shape of her mouth, her height. I wouldn't have pulled it out of the blue; but with the link made, I could see it. I said, "And now you wonder if the reason your mother split from here was because she was pregnant—and you think Jerry Corbin . . ."

There were tears in her eyes again, but they didn't fall. "I thought maybe he'd left her, but now I think it was she who left. Maybe she couldn't face her family, or she didn't love Jerry. I don't think he knew, which is why she never told me. But he must still *feel* something about her—he paid that unforeseen debt. He had no obligation to. My call yesterday confirmed that Ted Nash adopted me."

"And now you're wondering what to do with all this?"

She nodded and tears shook loose and rolled. I took her hand. "What do you feel about it?"

She tried to speak, couldn't, cleared her throat, and in a small voice said, "Confused. Scared. Afraid Jerry will reject me if I bring it up. But mostly, I feel like I'm . . . on the verge of solving a mystery of my own, one that might better be left alone."

She was looking at me, perhaps wanting me to tell her what to do. Her right eye had its own very slight outward tilt, and they were both a glimmering green.

"I'm not sure that's ever true," I said.

"Tonight is the show, and I've been all mixed up about this. That's why I was . . . why last night . . . " She gave up. A tear fell on my hand.

I drew a slow breath, trying to get my own thoughts clear. I said, "Only you can decide what you need to do. But you don't have to rush it. One thing at a time. Get through tonight first. Just that."

She sniffled and dried her eyes. She drank some coffee. When she had composed herself, she said, "What were you going to ask me about Justin?"

I smiled and shook my head. "Nothing you'd know anything about." I put down money for the check. "You've got fish to fry," I said. "And I've got some things to attend to, also."

"Will I see you later?"

I raised my right hand. "Sure you will."

At the elevator, she leaned up and planted a quick, only slightly tear-stained kiss on my jaw. I'd have taken it over an honorary doctorate any day.

26

I DROVE OUT Nesmith Street, then up Mansur to Belmont Avenue. There, in the lofty heights of old laissez-faire Lowell, I felt the city dwindling to insubstantiality behind me. This was Belvidere. No need for a leaf blower up here; except for occasional ancient beeches, still holding their coppery leaves, all the trees were evergreen. Like the bank accounts. Between the big homes I got glimpses of downtown far below. Washed in late-autumn sunlight, the city had the look of a toy town in a children's book illustration.

The Devlin ancestral castle was as easy to miss as Camelot, all stone and slate-scaled angles and red-brick chimneys, one of which breathed woodsmoke into the October sky. I parked in the circular cobblestone drive. The front door was fashioned from massive oak planks that all day with a battering ram might get you through. I used the ornate knocker in the form of a standing bear instead.

From the granite stoop I could peer over a privacy fence into an open area in front of a carriage house. There a big guy was buffing a deep blue Mercedes sedan with a chamois the size of a bed sheet. The car gleamed like wet midnight. The guy had the manner and look of a young Boog Powell, an effect enhanced by the plastic batting helmet and satin warm-up jacket he was wearing, both marked with the Orioles logo.

"You must be the cleanup batter," I called, giving him a winsome smile.

He quit buffing and turned a hard stare on me. "I'm the driver. Writing a book?"

Gone were the grand and glorious days of livery.

As I was about to give the knocker another go, the door opened. A short man with thinning gold hair and wearing a black suit peered past a sharp nose at me. "Yes, sir?" His was the same voice I'd gotten on the phone, with the kind of accent ski instructors affected.

"Mr. Devlin is expecting me," I said.

He nodded me in and asked me to wait. I didn't mind. I hadn't been in a museum in years. The room was baronial: ornate wood and plaster, geometric parquet, and oriental rugs as thick as lawn turf. In the corners trees grew from Chinese urns. At the far end was a wide, winding staircase, equipped with an escalator chair. The old paintings on the walls were depictions of fantastic mountains and wild landscapes.

"Would you come with me, sir," the man with the accent said. "Mr. Devlin will join you in the solarium."

We walked through the house quietly, which is the only way you can walk through a house like that. The solarium was in the southwest corner, filled with potted marigolds and geraniums, which spiced the air with a bitter, bracing smell. Three of the walls were leaded glass, in the center of each of which was a panel depicting the same bear-rampant figure as on the door knocker. Judy Bishop would probably know the heraldic meanings.

"Ah, Mr. Rasmussen," said someone behind me. "A pleasure."

I turned. I took the hand which Basil Devlin lifted off a cane. It was dry and liver spotted, but firm, which it would need to be to move around the cane: it looked like ebony. "A pleasure to meet *you,* sir," I said.

He still had the sensitive, fine-boned face I used to see often in the social and business pages of the newspapers, but he looked as though sickness had laid a dread hand on him. The ruddy look of lunches in the grillroom of the Vesper Country Club had faded. His mouth, the bags under his eyes, even his small white mustache looked tired. Everything but his eyes. His eyes were sharp and bright as an eagle's. I pegged him at eighty or very near. But never mind that, he was a presence in the city. The way his neighbor, former senator Paul Tsongas, was and would be for years to come. It's what Corbin meant by "juice."

Basil Devlin scowled up through one of the glass walls of the solarium. "I had hoped we could enjoy the sunshine as we chatted, but clouds are coming in. It'll be cold. Heinz, we'll use the sitting room."

I was ready to take off my jacket, but he was the host. I tagged along behind him and Heinz and climbed as Devlin rode the escalator chair to the second floor. "The weather's changing," he said. "We've mucked it up permanently." I thought about sharing with him the *Old Farmer's* forecast for later tonight and appearing oracular, but I figured he didn't need it. We reached the sitting room within the hour.

The walls were hung with more paintings, portraits of men in suits whose style went back through a century and more. All were posed with their hands on a book and looked important. "The family gallery," Devlin said with a wave. His was an old Anglo-Irish bloodline of farmers and bankers, a useful mix in the days when the Yankees were grudgingly letting go their stranglehold on local power. He nodded at a pair of chairs. No fear of sinking into these: they were fashioned of oak and leather and looked as if they had been upholstered by a taxidermist. We settled in before a limestone hearth, where a wood fire danced. When Heinz had gotten the old man settled, with the inevitable plaid lap blanket, he left us. Basil Devlin said, "I'm delighted you phoned, and that I can finally put a face to a name. I've heard about you around town."

"Nothing good, I hope."

The dewlaps creased in a small grin. "The man who accused you . . . Councilman Cavanaugh. A particularly loathsome species of fungus, I think. They seem to sprout at will in some of those shadowy corner offices of City Hall that seldom get swept. Of course, Devlins once occupied their share of said offices. But in those days there was no notion of careerism. What you had was a spirit of public service, of noblesse oblige."

"Which made a nice flip side to laissez-faire, if we're speaking French," I said. My bloodlines flowed from the working floor of the mills.

Devlin smiled. "Touché. I suppose that that spirit is one few can afford today. Still, I don't hold anything against any person who has a code that he tries to live by. You have one, haven't you, Mr. Rasmussen? A credo you operate under?"

The heat of the fire was making my face stiff. "I never put a name to it," I said.

"You have a reputation for reliable work."

"If I do a job so people are satisfied they got their money's worth, I get to keep on working. When I don't and they don't, it'll be time to close up shop and take a postal exam."

"Exactly the logic I used in recommending you to Jeremiah Corbin. He and I go way back, as he may have told you."

"He said his family worked for yours."

"For many years. A gentleman in his employ came, oh, two weeks ago, with a letter of introduction. Nice-looking man. Jewish, I believe."

"Justin Ross?"

"Ross, yes. He told me about Jeremiah's plans to visit the city. They were looking for someone to oversee security—someone unconnected with the police, he said. To minimize notoriety, I should think. People in the public eye must attract unwanted attention at times. Why, years ago—" Devlin sat back abruptly. "Forgive me. You're on a tight schedule. It's a big day for the city. And I'm just a paltry thing, a tattered coat upon a stick, whiling away the empty hours with talk."

"Somehow I don't think that's ever described you, sir."

"Thank you. What can I do for you?"

He was right. Time was in limited supply. "I know that you went to Harvard," I said. "I'm looking for a little help. Were you familiar with the clubs there?"

His eyes brightened. "I was Pork," he said. My face must have shown my confusion. "Porcellian," he explained. "It's one of the oldest and most respected."

I nodded. "Did you ever hear of an unofficial club whose members swore an oath to uphold the traditions of the school and itself?"

Devlin touched his mustache. "Hmm—most of them have oaths of one sort or another."

"This would've been to do anything necessary, including take revenge."

For a moment he made no response. Flames muttered in the hearth. Then he said, "You know of this club?"

"Hearsay only, sir. Does such a club exist?"

His gaze seemed to turn inward. One hand fumbled at the plaid blanket and drew it higher. The other gripped the chair arm. Except for his eyes, the gnarled hands appeared to be the only part of him that was vital. "Did exist," he said. "In rumor, at least. It was strictly . . . beyond the pale. The story was that there was a club which had its origins among the grandsons of men who had come to this continent in prison ships."

"As criminals?" I asked.

"It was common practice in the colonies. And, as history suggests, our good fortune. It's often the qualities of cunning, daring, resourcefulness—a willingness to *stretch* the limits?—that have led men to achieve and society to benefit." It was a variation on his free-market riff, but I was patient. After a moment's ramble, he found the original topic again. "Over time, the heirs of some of those convicts managed to find themselves matriculating at Harvard College. There, to defend their names against the inevitable calumny if their ancestry were learned, several purportedly banded together. This would have been in the early eighteenth century. Of course, this is sketchy history."

He paused, his breathing having become harder. I glanced toward the oxygen tank. He saw my glance and shook his head. He went on. "The story was that clubmen were handpicked. And each was sworn to a code such as you describe—to avenge wrong done to any other member. Recall, these men would have had some criminal blood in their veins, so the notion was that vengeance could be cruel." His faint smile said he was playing along. "It makes a good story. I doubt college records would substantiate it. In fact, I'm sure Harvard would pointedly *deny* the club's existence."

He started to cough. Heinz came in and got the oxygen mask ready, but Devlin ignored it. After a moment the coughing subsided, but I didn't want to push it. I rose. "Would you happen to know the name of the club, sir?"

For a moment I thought he hadn't heard me, or didn't understand the question. Then, absently, his hand rose again to finger his small mustache. He said, "The club, yes. It was called Crossbones."

I thanked Devlin for his hospitality. He stayed seated as we shook hands.

"Give my good wishes to Jeremiah," he said. "He invited me to attend tonight's event. Unfortunately, my social life between now and next April will be reserved for Palm Beach. We'll be leaving tomorrow. I don't do well with the cold." He managed a smile. "When you get to my age, you realize there are people dying who never died before, and you take care." He lifted a grizzled hand. "Have a good winter, Mr. Rasmussen."

Heinz showed me to the door. When I got outside, I filled my lungs several times with the cool autumn air.

* * *

My office was on the way to the Riverfront Plaza, and I pulled into the adjacent alley and parked. Upstairs I got a number from my notebook and dialed it. As the other end rang, I unlocked a drawer in my file cabinet and took out the Smith & Wesson K-38 Masterpiece that was half-lifing in there. I checked the load. I put it into the snap-holster and fastened the holster on my belt. Justin Ross would be happy. I was about to hang up the phone when Missy Pickering answered. We chatted a moment about the impending end of Indian summer. Then her husband got on another phone and Missy hung up.

"Yes, what's up?" Noel Pickering asked.

"Try a name for me," I said and gave it.

There was a silence on the line, and I thought I could hear the moan of a foghorn off the Cohasset coast. I wondered if Pickering was in his studio, painting viscera. Then he said, "Well, what do you know? An old sawbones like me, and I'd forgotten that. Sure, the club Tom Chapman belonged to was Crossbones."

27

Phil Gripaldi answered the hotel room door wearing a tuxedo. He blushed. "I know. I look like kinda normal, huh?"

"Fifty-inch chests are everywhere," I said. "Is Chelsea in?"

"She's over at the U. already. I'm waiting on Mr. C. Come on in."

The suite had an expectant energy: people adjusting cummerbunds, flapping pages of script. I didn't see any champagne, but there was a bottle of Pepto-Bismol on a table. I went back to the bedroom and knocked. Corbin sat at a dressing table with a napkin around his neck as a makeup girl brushed his face. His eyes met mine in the mirror.

"Jesus, Rasmussen, you going like that? Where's your tux?"

"I had to return it after the senior prom." I said, "Let's talk about this."

He drew the napkin off his neck and thanked the girl, who took her kit and went out. I shut the door behind her. "I think you should cancel," I said.

"Sure, no problem. Cancel the show. Are you crazy? It's two hours from now! It's sold out."

I replayed my conversation with Basil Devlin about Crossbones. Corbin scowled the whole time. "One of the Harvard quiz group was a member," I said.

"Yeah, a guy who's dead. I'm getting sick of this. Fun is fun, but this has gone way too far. There've been opportunities to make trouble before now, and nothing's happened. Someone was yanking my chain. It's over."

"Maybe that's the idea."

"What do you mean?"

"Tonight's the show. Maybe it comes down to tonight."

"Forget it. The show is on."

I said, "I could change that."

"What are you talking about?"

I had my back to the closed door. "You've still got to get to the auditorium."

He shook his head, trying a grin. "Gripaldi's out there. You want to tangle with him?"

"Wouldn't have to. I've got this." I opened my jacket to show him the butt of the .38 on my belt.

"You work for me, damn it!"

"That's kind of how I figure it, too," I said. "The stock on my shelf is my ability to deliver. Okay, we've kept all this off the news. The other idea was I'm supposed to protect you."

Corbin chewed the implications of that for a moment, then shook his head. "Cancellation isn't an option. It never has been. Too many people are counting on this. The show is on." He got up. "You gonna shoot me?"

It had been worth a try. I shook my head. "I can't. You've still got my retainer."

Corbin forced a grin. "You'll be there, and Gripaldi, and the cops. Plus I've got my dynamite material. I'll knock 'em dead."

In the outer room, Gripaldi told me that Chelsea was on the phone. She wanted to speak with me. I went into the alcove where the fax machine was and took the call. "How's it going?" I said.

"Much better. I've decided to talk with Jerry, but after the show. He's got enough on his mind without worrying whether he's got a bastard daughter." Her laugh sounded nervous. "How are you?"

"Happy that you're happy," I said.

"Thanks. Did Justin get hold of you?"

"When?"

"A couple hours ago? He told me he'd call you before going over to see Professor Westrake."

"I haven't been at my office."

"He's convinced it's Westrake who's been sending those messages." She paused. "Is he right?"

"I don't know. I'll come over there."

"Westrake's not here. Justin was going out to his house."

"Where's that?"

"Wait." I heard pages rattle, then she gave me a phone number and an address far out on Pawtucket Boulevard. "Good luck, Alex. I've got to go. See you tonight."

I dialed Westrake's home number, but I got Ma Bell telling me the line was not in service at this time. As I broke the connection, about to call Ed St. Onge, I got another one of my funny notions. Call it intuition—or curiosity. Possibly it was paranoia. I unscrewed the mouthpiece of the receiver. Nested among the colored wires, stuck to the diaphragm with a magnet, was a little extra widget that didn't belong to Ma Bell. I picked it out and examined it in the light. I didn't need an entomology book to identify it.

28

Ten minutes later, I was picking my way out Pawtucket Boulevard, trying to get some running room in the 6:00 rush. The clocks would fall back tonight, and tomorrow it would be dark as a pocket at this hour; now, though, there was still fading light. A glow in the mist above the river foretold where the full moon would shortly rise. In the side streets I could make out the early flit of witches and ghosts. I found myself thinking about the night in the Copper Kettle when Justin Ross had hired me, the fog pressing against the barroom window, red-stained with neon. All of this had begun in mist. I wondered how it would end.

At a stoplight, I slipped the bug out of my pocket and looked at it again. It appeared to be a miniature radio transmitter. It hadn't swayed Corbin one bit. If anything, his bravado had grown. But I understood why he would scoff at the notion of someone eavesdropping on his conversations, sending him kook mail, stalking him. He had to. He was afraid of a subtler enemy; one with a Nielsen report in one hand, and a remote channel control in the other. If I could have I'd like to have laid everything out for him, even if just to hear it said; but he wasn't listening. And who else was there? Justin Ross? Chelsea? St. Onge? It would take too long, and it wouldn't make any sense. It didn't make enough sense to me. Yet I believed that everything was connected: from Florence Murphy to the college quiz bowl, the Crossbones Club to the Canal Club, to the little voice-activated bug in the phone in Corbin's suite, and to Alfred Westrake, too—links that needed only to be assembled in the right order to become a chain that stretched from some old past and was trying to reach down the years to tonight. I had told Corbin, "Break a leg."

Westrake's house was out beyond the city waterworks, set back from the road, along the riverbank. I drew in front and shut off the headlights and motor. Dusk was full now. The house was a bungalow, brown maybe, or dark gray, with a light burning somewhere inside. At the far end of the driveway, there was a car in front of a garage. A wind had risen, and the yard seemed to be in motion, filling with drifted leaves. I went to the front door and knocked.

The moon was up, fat and waxy yellow beyond the dark line of trees on the other side of the river. My knocking raised no one. I tried the knob and discovered the door was unlocked. That gave me a moment's pause. Then I pushed open the door and called Westrake's name. Nothing. I yelled Justin Ross's name. Silence. My heart beat a little faster.

Another man might have gone home then and listened to one of those AM radio call-in shows with advice about investing for the future. Or he would dole out candy for the neighborhood trick-or-treaters, then instruct the baby-sitter and bundle his wife into the minivan and go catch Jerry Corbin and laugh with his fellow citizens and forget for a while that there was trouble in the world at all. I lifted my weapon out of its holster and stepped inside the silent house.

I shut the door. The light was coming through from another room, just enough to see by. The bungalow was small, but even so, each room I came to was given over to books. Hundreds of them, arrayed on shelves, heaped on every available surface, erected like barrier reefs against the tides of change. They lent the house their weight and their musty aroma. It was testimony to Westrake's mania that even the kitchen had been converted to simply more book space. It was there that the lamps were lighted; one over the sink, the other on a table against a wall. The table did double duty as an eating surface and a work desk, but it was far messier than either one should have been. And I saw why. It had been searched hastily. Notes and correspondence, student blue books, academic journals, and the incomplete manuscripts of scholarly works lay scattered amid upset salt and pepper shakers and teacups. An overturned ashtray had spilled the stubs of dead cigars.

I put my gun away.

Among the papers I found a journal. It was one of those old booklets with a marbleized paper cover. Handwritten across the front was "Diary of Shame." I skimmed pages. The journal told of how in the early 1950s, while Westrake was a lecturer at Harvard, a small group of students had mounted a campaign of lies and false witness, charging him with treasonous ideas and "academic turpitude," whatever that was.

What had been only fragments of meaning were coming together in my mind, an incomplete picture emerging that was far different than what I had begun to assume. I fanned more pages and found a photograph.

The picture was the same, or a duplicate, of one Westrake had shown me in his office, of the old quiz-bowl team—except with a change. In red marker pen, someone had drawn horns on young Jerry Corbin. Devil's horns.

My heart had begun to bang with a more insistent tempo. I went back to the front room and picked up the phone. Time to get St. Onge. The receiver made no sound. I followed the cord and saw why. Cut.

As I stepped outside, a gust of wind lashed at me. Turning away from it, I peered up the dark driveway. What I had taken before as a garage, I saw now was actually a small cabin.

I got a flashlight out of my car. Walking back toward the cabin, I came to the car in the driveway and realized this was the third time I had seen it. The second time had been two nights ago, when it had tried to run me down in a parking lot. In the windshield was a crack that my bottle of gin had made. Satisfying myself that there wasn't a skeleton at the wheel, I opened the driver-side door. The ignition wires were twisted together and taped. There were some audiocassettes on the console: Black Flag, Sick of It All, Suicidal Tendencies . . . music no seventy-five-year-old scholar would be into, no matter how hip. I eased the Camaro's door closed and went on past.

Though I couldn't see it, the cabin's rear had to be pitched right on the bank of the Merrimack. The water was a slick blackness beyond. I knocked on the door. When no one came, I tried the knob. This one was locked. I directed my light through a door pane and stooped to look in. The place was small—three rooms, I figured. Gripping the knob tightly and twisting, I rammed the door with my shoulder. It moved as much as the Patriots' offense. I took out my no-knock warrant. Holding the walnut grip, I tapped the three-inch barrel against the pane above the knob. Glass tinkled in. I holstered the .38, reached through and turned the deadbolt. For the second time in ten minutes, I performed criminal trespass.

I flipped a wall switch, but got nothing. My flashlight picked out scant furnishings. A worn-out couch. A TV. On a coffee table lay an open book. There was a passage underlined in red marker pen.

Full fathom five thy father lies,
Of his bones are coral made.
Those are pearls that were his eyes,
Nothing of him that doth fade
But doth suffer a sea-change

Into something rich and strange.
Sea-nymphs hourly ring his knell:
Ding-dong.
Hark, now I hear them—Ding-dong bell.

The book was Shakespeare's *The Tempest.* An impression stirred at the edge of my memory and I tried to get hold of it; but just then the flashlight beam lit something standing upright in a doorway. A boot. I went over and picked it up. I ran my fingers over little bumps in the leather.

I had never touched ostrich skin before.

I shone the light into the next room and saw someone sitting there in the dark, facing a wood stove. He had one bare foot propped on a stool, as if he'd taken the boot and sock off to warm his toes. Except the stove was cold.

I said Justin Ross's name. The person didn't turn. I stepped closer. His head glimmered. There was a clear plastic bag over it, cinched in place with his bolo tie, puckered where his last breath had sucked it into the O of his mouth. I peered through the fogged plastic to be sure it was Ross. It was. I touched him. He was as cold as the stove.

My mind frayed out for a moment . . . then came back. Touching nothing else, I examined him visually. He was handcuffed to the arms of the chair. On the back of one hand was a small red circle that puzzled me a moment until I found several others on the sole of his bare foot. They were scorch wounds, like a hot poker or a lighted cigar might make. I felt sick, unnerved at the knowledge that my delays had brought things to this. As I pondered my failings, the darkness on one side of me moved. I whirled. The flashlight lit a face: wild-eyed, long-haired, white with ghostly suddenness. Westrake. His hand was up in what I thought was a wave, but that was only more dumb thinking. The arm dropped, and before I could react, something tore into my chest.

The flashlight sprang from my hand. I rode a shock wave, trying to stay on it, to stay up; then my legs were gone. For just an instant, I stared sideways into a circle of light, then it was nowhere.

29

I WOKE FACEDOWN in darkness, pain a dull presence in my chest. I lay on a hard surface. As I moved, my cheek came unglued from the surface with a sticky sound. I rolled onto my left side. The effort made my chest thud. Dimly I was aware that there was something I needed to do, a place I should be, but for the life of me I couldn't recollect what it was.

Using my hands, I managed to get to a sitting position. I was on a floor. As I felt around me, my hand bumped something, spinning it. My flashlight. I turned it on. The floor was smeared with blood: not too much of it, but what's too much? The front of my shirt was wet with it, too. With careful fingers, I probed inside my shirt. There was a wound in my chest, but evidently lying on it had slowed the bleeding to an ooze.

In the light's glow I saw a few snippets of copper wire and a length of cloth on the floor. The cloth was damp. Nearby lay an eighteen-inch piece of aluminum tube. Something wanted to come into my memory, but I couldn't grab it.

My watch said it was after 7:00. A chunk of time was gone. Taking more of it, I got to my feet. I made my way to the kitchen and splashed cold water on my face, wiping at the blood on my cheek. Bits of the past came back. Westrake stabbing me with a metal tube. And . . .

I shone the light behind me.

Like a watcher in the dark, Justin Ross peered out of the fogged plastic bag. I clapped at the .38 on my waist: still there. But I'd been asleep on the job. I went over. Justin was a long way from sunshine and palm trees. I wanted to loosen the bolo tie from his throat, remove the bag, take the cuffs off his wrists, speak with him, drive him down to the Copper Kettle, buy him a non-alcohol drink. But I couldn't. I touched nothing.

I got outside. The Camaro was gone. I walked to my car carefully, like a man wanting to keep something from spilling. Just climbing in, shutting the door, gripping the wheel, shifting the gears . . . every movement was an effort. In some small way, I welcomed the glitter of pain each brought, as if it were my due for having screwed up. As I got out onto Route 113, I saw flashing lights approaching. I didn't stop. A cruiser sped past in a blur of red and blue. I blinked my vision into focus. I switched on the radio, and began poking the channel presets, trying to remember which station was carrying *The New Gong Show.* Disembodied voices drifted out like ghosts before I remembered *television*—not radio—and I snapped it off.

The shoulder above my chest wound was stiffening. Pain had settled into a jagged ache, making movement difficult. Thoughts came randomly: bits of wire and aluminum, Shakespeare, Westrake's diary, darkness. I shouldn't be driving. How much blood had I lost? Lowell General wasn't far away—should I go there? Or try to get St. Onge? Too late. If he figured I'd tried to end-run him, I wasn't going to have to worry anymore about losing my P.I. license. Somehow none of that bothered me. It was all just mind noise.

When I came to the turnoff for the hospital, I kept going.

I opened the window, wanting air to clear my head. What I got were voices: *You bozo, Rasmussen, you should've seen this coming. But no, you were too busy finessing your theories of guilt and motivation. Busy planking the boss's daughter. And now Justin Ross was dead, maybe tortured before he'd died, your own life almost snatched by an old man with a piece of aluminum tube, and you're spinning radio dials when you should be doing . . . going . . .* I jerked the wheel as the car started to veer off the road. I gulped cold air.

Aluminum tube, damp cloth, copper wire . . . the details kept nagging. Full fathom five . . .

As I neared the university campus, traffic thickened. There were cars parking along both sides of the road. I was still a half-mile from the college auditorium. Jerry Corbin might be dog meat to the industry hacks, but he still had pulling power with the people of Lowell.

I managed another hundred yards before a campus cop waving a pink wand barred the way. He wanted me to exit into a parking lot. I motioned that I needed to pass, but that got me nowhere. I did as he said. I got my trench coat out of the car. I dragged it on over my bloodied shirt, turned up the collar. I stuffed the flashlight into one pocket. I put my gun in the other. I put on my hat. Each task dizzied me.

There was a flow of people on the sidewalk. Older folks, mostly, the same ones you saw Sunday afternoons at the free lectures at the War Memorial Auditorium, but they had anted up tonight. Some were in costume, and I remembered the show was also a party. The thought didn't thrill me, but for the moment it was okay. I got in among them, and nobody looked twice. Bogie was cool. Here's looking at you, kid.

On campus there were more uniforms, both the university and the city variety. It was Halloween; maybe the cops weren't cops. If they were, I could stop, hope to convince them I was on the level, that Corbin was at risk. Except what if they wanted to take me to a hospital first, or downtown, put the questions to me, like why had I kept them in the dark so long? Why hadn't I reported finding Ross's body? Where was I going with a rod in my pocket? Just who the hell did I think I was anyway? The clock on the campus bell tower showed 7:51.

The foot traffic began to slow. Conversations were full of anticipation and excitement. I glanced to my left, looking for passing room. That's when I spotted someone moving across the quadrangle there, into the darkness, away from the crowd. He was garbed as a warlock, maybe, or a monk, and it took me a few more strides to realize that it wasn't a costume but a coat with a hood drawn up and that I had seen the getup before.

I stepped away from the lighted walk and started across the grass, after him. I didn't yell out this time the way I had the night I'd spotted him coming out of Alumni Hall and had given chase. I didn't like the idea of moving too quickly—it made me think of blood flowing—but I had to get to him.

He was moving along at a purposeful clip, unaware of me. I saw him go around a building, and then I was alone in the dark, my feet shuffling in the rug of pine needles. I quickened my own pace, but you could've completed a master's program by the time I rounded the corner. Even so, I was panting. As I reached the rear of the auditorium, I looked for the man in the hood, but he was gone. The only thing between me and the building was a large trailer van, marked with the NBC peacock. It was hooked to the auditorium with electrical cables, as if it was giving the building a jump start. As I got near, I could hear it hum. When I got there, I used the handrail and went up a flight of portable metal steps and opened the trailer door.

The interior was narrow and dimly lit. A handful of people sat at a long control panel, staring at a lot of little TV screens. Most wore headphones. The woman who didn't turned my way.

"Hey," she said. "This is off-limits."

I looked for the man I had been chasing. The cool air felt good. I closed my eyes.

"Mister . . . Hey, are you sick or something? You look kinda pale."

I wiped a hand over my face and brought it away damp. "Naw, I'm just—"

One of the screens showed the cowled figure jogging toward some bushes. The action was in black-and-white. I watched, disoriented. "Where's that?"

The TV woman looked confused. "What?"

"That screen." I pointed. "Where is it?"

"I don't know. Look, you're gonna have to—"

"Where *is* it?"

"It's a roving camera." She addressed the others: "Where's four?" One of the technicians spoke into his microphone. "Four, what's your location?"

Then the camera roved more, and I recognized what it was aimed at. I lurched out of the trailer and down the steps. The woman called something after me, but I didn't turn.

It seemed a very long distance to where the man in the hood had just been. No one was around when I got there. A wind was rising, swirling leaves. The air was colder. I went through the bushes I'd seen on the monitor. My eyes had grown used to the darkness. Beyond the thicket, I crunched down a weedy slope. A branch took off my hat, and I reached for it but missed. I didn't stop. At the bottom was the building I had recognized on TV. I found the door and opened it. Heat lapped across me like a dragon's breath. I stepped into the steam plant.

A memory thawed, like the tip of a mastodon tusk coming out of the ice: fuh, fuh, fuh . . . the sounds that had murdered my sleep two nights ago . . . the voice on the telephone. *F*ull *f*athom *f*ive thy *f*ather lies. *Shakespeare?*

Ahead I saw the faint glow from the old boiler-tender's little pack rat's nest. One of his bumper stickers was pasted on the wall. KEEP IT SIMPLE. Okay, good advice. Find the furnace man, have him guide me through the tunnels to the cellar entrance to the auditorium, locate Chelsea and get word to Corbin: hold the show, find St. Onge, screw the delays, in the long run it would build interest, and it would mean America could go on laughing with Jerry Corbin, because he'd be alive.

EASY DOES IT, urged another sign.

"Hey," I said, remembering I'd startled the old fellow the last time. Curtis *Smyth.* With a *y.* I called it out. No response. Then I realized he'd be up in the auditorium in a secondhand jacket and tie with the complimentary pass we'd sent him. I stepped around the boiler.

Smyth's Philco was playing softly. Smyth himself was lounging just out of the spill of lamplight in his overstuffed chair, heeding the AA message. I gripped his shoulder. "Didn't you get—?"

His head lolled sideways. I stepped around to face him—*and recoiled.* Then I saw it was a rubber mask drawn over his head. A skull mask. I pulled it off. The face underneath was worse—because it was real. The flesh was purple; the eyes bulged. A twist of copper wire had cut off his final breath.

In my line of sight, just beyond Smyth's head, another of his signs said ONE DAY AT A TIME. But the days had run out. I switched off the radio, perhaps to give him peace, and I heard another sound. A shuffle of footsteps on concrete. I turned. The lamp threw a moving shadow. A gunshot exploded. The round whined off the cast-iron boiler. I was falling to the floor as a second bullet *chunked* into a furnace duct with a puff of dust. Grit sifted down onto my head. Asbestos. I'd probably contract cancer in thirty years. But I wasn't worrying about cancer, or about thirty years from now. I was thinking of right this minute, one second at a time. The gun sounded like a cannon.

I worked my own out of my coat pocket. I scrabbled forward to where I could point it up at the lamp, and squeezed. The room went dark. Echoes of my shot rang away to silence. I lay there in it, my heart drumming against my breastbone so hard I worried that my wound would start bleeding again. But somewhere in the darkness was the killer, and that worried me more.

He had struck boldly, and though his pattern suggested intelligence, there was the thread of madness woven through it. Apparently, he was unafraid of anything; intent only on the one goal he'd been intent on the whole time, starting with that first note and running right through all the weirdness to now. He wanted to kill Jerry Corbin.

And what stood between him and Corbin—and whoever else he would take down in the process—was me.

With a finger I squeegeed sweat off my brow. I crept forward on the insides of my forearms and thighs. The low crawl, we used to call it in the army. It had never been one of my favorite sports, and it was even less so now on the cold, dusty concrete, with a rip in my chest and a maniac nearby, looking to kill me.

I heard a shuffle of footsteps and I fired. My gun muzzle sparked in the darkness.

More sound, diminishing along the tunnel. I lay still until a door creaked open at the far end, light flared, and the door slammed shut, taking the light. I got up. I dug out my flashlight.

I looked at Curtis Smyth. I probed the wrinkled folds of flesh beneath his chin. He hadn't been dead long. I was one campfire behind his killer, perhaps had been for days and hadn't known it; and I still didn't know for sure who he was. On the floor by the side of Smyth's chair was a small envelope of the kind that tickets come in. I picked it up. *All my best!* was handwritten on the outside, and it was signed *Jerry Corbin.* It was empty.

At the end of the long tunnel I came to a metal-sheathed door. I got it open, peered in, and went through as fast as I could manage, ready with the .38. Another length of tunnel, this one dimly lit with overhead bulbs, some of them burned out. It forked in two directions, both empty. Stenciled on the cinder-block wall were a pair of pointing hands. One aimed left, with KITCHENS underneath. The other aimed right. AUD. and ALUM. HALL the faded words under it said, and another little piece fell into place. The night I had surprised the murderer coming out of Alumni Hall, he had been down in these tunnels. Which raised another question. Why?

I went right. I could tell by the dust in them that the tunnels were little used. I was thinking again of wire and tubing, trying to make them come together. Overhead I heard a noise, and I twitched the flashlight beam upward. Among the cobwebs and the medieval slither of shadows shone a length of new aluminum tubing. I puzzled on that for a moment and then remembered the little artifact of tubing and wire that Curtis Smyth had found on the floor the night I'd met him. I thought I should go back and see where the overhead tubing began, but I didn't have time. The noise I heard above me was the sound of people. I was nearing the auditorium.

I went on, pointing the light up every few yards to see if the tubing was still there. It was. I was under the auditorium now. I could feel the vibration of movement above, the pulse of a crowd. The flashlight picked up a little gleam on the cement floor ahead. I bent and saw it was a splash of lead solder. I pondered that a second, then shone the light straight up. The tubing ended there, and from it several strands of electrical wiring ran up through the ceiling. And then I knew.

I got to a door marked AUDITORIUM. I reached for the handle and pulled. Right, like I expected it to swing open on its counterweights to a trumpet fanfare. It didn't budge. Above me I heard feet stamping on the floor, applause.

I checked my watch and felt my heart sink.

8:00 P.M.

Show time.

30

I KEPT UP a steady pounding on the metal-sheathed door. After a long moment, it opened. A heavyset campus cop stood there.

"Did someone just come through?" I asked, guessing the answer, guessing where Curtis Smyth's ticket had gone.

"Who the hell are you?"

Explanations were going to take too long. I managed to get out my license. When the cop stopped laughing, he handed it back. "Nice try, skipper. All right, back the way you came and buy a ticket like everybody else."

"That's for real," I said. "There's a dead man back in—"

"And you're Sam Spade." He started to close the door, but I blocked it with my foot. "Christ, what is it, the full moon?" he said. "Take a hike!" He put a hand on my chest and shoved.

I staggered a step backward, wincing with pain, but managed a grin. "Okay, I can't fool you," I said. "The problem is at central casting they ran out of toy guns. They gave me this."

Nearsighted bank tellers and old parties in mom-and-pop stores can sometimes think a squirt gun is the real thing; but it never works the other way. When the campus cop pulled his eyes off the blue-steel barrel of the .38, he was putty in my hands. I got him into the steam tunnel and locked him out. Holstering my gun, I oriented myself, saw I was in the backstage area of the auditorium. I was getting close. I went down an adjoining corridor. I went through a door. Several heads turned.

"Hey! Rasmussen!" It was Gus Deemys. "Hold it!"

Maybe I'd have tried to tell another cop, but not Deemys. I ducked out.

"Sonofa—*Hey!*" Deemys shouted. "Someone grab that bastard!"

I started to run along the corridor. I wasn't sure where I was, or where I needed to be. I turned into another doorway, into a darkened room, and stumbled. Cables and wires snaked across the floor. The hookup to the broadcast truck in back. I followed the cables past a partition and emerged in the auditorium. I was near the front. The house lights were down but I could see that every seat was filled and people were standing in the back. The stage was lighted and TV cameras hovered at the dim edges. The set I had seen yesterday was occupied with actors, and there was one addition. A big ornate metal gong hung from a stand at center stage.

Then I saw something which rooted me to the spot. Jerry Corbin, in his tuxedo, was moving toward the gong with a steel mallet.

I stepped toward the stairs and shouted his name. He looked startled, then his face tightened in what had to be anger. Here I was torpedoing his debut, and not even wearing a tux! He glanced suddenly toward the side.

The curtain was flung aside. A cowled figure charged out, gun in hand. Before I could react, there was a blur of motion from the wings: the tuxedoed bulk of Gripaldi. The man in the cowl whirled and fired. Gripaldi went down as if a barbell had dropped on him. The auditorium erupted with screams.

Corbin threw aside the mallet and went to Gripaldi. Chelsea rushed out, too. As I struggled up the stage stairs, the man in the cowl grabbed Chelsea.

I left my gun where it was. Corbin stood up. He stepped toward the cowled figure. I still couldn't see a face.

"You want to talk about this, okay," Corbin said. He was miked and his voice went through the auditorium. "You and I. I'll listen. But whoever the hell you are, or whatever this is, it's got nothing to do with her. Let her go." Jerry turned to the audience, his face red and sweating. "Everyone be calm!" he commanded. Cops had materialized in the wings, their hands on their guns. The red lights told me the cameras were on, catching it all.

Corbin was walking forward carefully. I was, too; up the stairs, just out of the glow of lights, stepping over cables, looking for an angle, praying no one would panic.

Corbin was closer. As he took another step, the man in the cowl flung Chelsea down. He grabbed Corbin by his lapels and started to swing him around. I wasn't as near as I wanted to be, but time had run out. I lunged. My momentum knocked Corbin aside. I tackled the man in the hood. I tried to pull him down, but he yanked free, kicking at me. Stumbling, he lifted the .45 and fired. His backward motion took him into the gong.

There was an explosive *pop*. For an instant, the juice drained from the stage lights, washing the scene in a sickish glow. Then they blazed back fully.

Spotlighted at center stage, right where he had hoped Jerry Corbin would be when he banged the gong with the mallet, was the person in the cowl. He was spread-eagled against the steel disk. His coat smoked. His mouth gaped wide in a grin of horror as his skin started to blacken up around it like burning paper.

The whole place went dark.

Emergency lights came on, revealing: Jerry hugging Chelsea. The show's guests on their feet, frozen. Gripaldi being attended to by cops.

Alone, at the base of the gong, lay the stalker. I went over and squatted by him. For a moment, I did nothing; then I peeled back the scorched hood. Even under the blackened flesh and singed hair, I knew the face. I had seen it once before. Not the night I had pursued him across campus and he had eluded me, or when he had tried to run me down in the supermarket parking lot. Nor had I connected it with the voice on the telephone calling to frighten me away with obscure references to his own personal drama, or with the cast-off belongings stored in boxes at Eliot House at Harvard. No, it was an age or two ago, the time we had chatted amiably in the mild autumn sunshine as I had helped him carry stage-prop columns across campus. I could almost feel sympathy for this poor crazy kid who must've had such hostility and conflict about his father for leaving him, and yet had been drawn into the man's sick fantasy of vengeance for imagined crimes. I could *almost* feel sympathy, but I didn't.

I looked away. He didn't need a monster mask.

31

THE COPS GOT the crowd cleared out; power was restored; the show's special guests departed; paramedics arrived—none of this in any particular order that I was aware of. A bald man with a mustache made me sit on the stage as he snipped open my shirt and checked my wound. I was lucky, he said. There was a ragged puncture in the chest muscle, but nothing worse. He'd get it cleaned and dressed for me in a moment. I asked about Gripaldi and was told he was on his way to the hospital. Corbin came over with Ed St. Onge and Gus Deemys. St. Onge looked at me. "You got something to say?"

"I'd like to thank the members of . . . " I let it go. I didn't feel comedic.

"Are you all right?" Jerry Corbin said.

I nodded.

"Anyone know who the dead guy is?" St. Onge asked.

Corbin shook his head. "No idea."

I said, "The name Thomas Chapman ring a bell?"

The makeup on Corbin's forehead was streaked, giving the look of deep furrows. He added real ones. "He was on the Harvard quiz team, ages ago. But that isn't—"

"Chapman's dead," I said. "Died in a sailboat. That's his son."

"There're connections to me?"

"Only weird ones, in his own mind. He was an electronics whiz. He wired up that gong to fry you when you hit it."

"Damn."

"Probably would've won you a posthumous Emmy."

"Damn."

"Probably has an activator in his pocket."

St. Onge motioned with his head for Deemys to check. Deemys came back with a tiny black box with a button in the middle. "He wanted to be sure it was you," I told Corbin, "and not the dog-food lady."

St. Onge said, "He stab you?"

"Westrake did. He was tied and gagged at the kid's place, behind Westrake's house. He'd gotten loose, and when he heard me come in . . . it was dark; he panicked."

"Where is he now?"

I said I didn't know, but it came to me that I did know. Over the years, Westrake's life had become reefed in by books, and although in the end they had offered him no real protection, there was nothing else. "Try his office. But go easy. He's more confused than dangerous. His only sins go back too many years to matter."

St. Onge looked at me a moment, then followed Deemys out. Reluctantly, I told Jerry that Justin Ross was dead. He whispered something, sat down heavily, and said nothing more. The paramedic with the mustache returned. He said Gripaldi was a lucky guy, too; the gunshot wound was a clean one, no serious damage. The paramedic opened a plastic box and took out a pair of pool cues fashioned to look like hypodermic needles. St. Onge came back. "I sent Deemys over to get Westrake. We also found Ross. Looks like he might've been tortured before he was strangled."

"With a soldering iron, I think. To find out if Jerry knew about tonight," I said.

St. Onge nodded. "Then the kid took Ross's rental car."

"Yeah, and left behind the stolen Camaro I asked you about. How Westrake got here, I guess. In the campus steam plant there's one more person to account for." I told him about Curtis Smyth.

St. Onge took notes with a grim expression, then he said, "You played loose with this. We had a deal."

I found nothing to say.

"I'm gonna need your weapon."

I let him take it. He knocked out the cylinder, peered into the chambers, drew the weapon close to his nose, and sniffed. I didn't need to tell him it had been fired. He closed it and put it into his jacket pocket.

"If you'd talked to me, it's possible we might've stopped some of this," St. Onge said.

The truth of the words was sharper than the needle that pricked my arm. I could have told him I didn't know enough until it was too late, but what did it change? Three people were dead, and nothing was going to alter that. I didn't say anything.

"That one's tetanus," the paramedic explained. "With a puncture wound, you're better safe than sorry."

"God forbid Rasmussen gets lockjaw," St. Onge said.

As the paramedic thumbed the plunger on the second syringe, St. Onge looked away.

"What about my gun?" I said.

"It'll go to a lab, to assure me no one got dead by it. You won't be operating any heavy machinery tonight." He fitted a cigarette into a corner of his mouth where it bounced, unlit, as he spoke. "If you're up to it in the morning, you can give your complete version. Don't plan on basking in the limelight though. Lieutenant Droney's already there, beaming for the cameras, weaving fables about the glorious exploits of Lowell's finest, making the city safe for a favorite son." St. Onge shook hands with Jerry Corbin and went out.

Jerry was saying something to me, but the words were mush

in my head. My brow was clammy all at once. Everything began to spin. I pressed tighter in the chair, but it didn't slow things down. I was on a wild carousel. Faces around me started to fuzz, and the stage lights ran together. Then there was no light or time, just voices, faint and far, far away, part of a background—*Alex . . . Alex . . . Alex . . .* Except I was someplace too interesting, a place of color, movement, and sensation that would engage me to the end of forever. *Alex . . . Alex . . .*

But something went wrong. Or right. I didn't want to be there forever. The voices moved out of the background.

"Alex!"

I turned the focus wheel and saw haloed forms bending over me. Corbin and the paramedic and Chelsea were squatting there. Chelsea had a cool compress on my brow. My head was on something soft. "Welcome back, tough guy," Jerry Corbin said.

I looked at them. "I was out?"

"About a minute there. We managed to catch you before you hit the deck. How do you feel?"

"Like I had my hat blocked, with me wearing it."

"What hat?" Corbin said.

The paramedic folded up his stethoscope. "Just a delayed reaction. Your blood pressure's coming back, and your signs are fine."

I sat up slowly. The pillow, I saw, was Corbin's tux jacket. They helped me to my feet. The floor didn't cave under me. The paramedic said, "I gave you morphine. It'll knock the edge off your pain, but when it does, it's gonna be like someone dumped a hod of bricks off a scaffold on you."

"Nothing new," I mumbled.

"It'll take a little while, but then you're gonna sleep."

I thanked him, and he left.

"Want some water?" Jerry asked. "Or coffee?"

I shook my head. After a moment he went over to the side of

the stage to deal with some TV people. Chelsea took my arm. As a testament to her continuing good taste, she was costumed as nobody but herself. She had on a Black Watch kilt, with a big gold pin in it, and a black cowl-neck sweater, and her glasses. New pennies glinted from her loafers. "You're sure you're feeling okay?"

"Like a million," I said, wincing as she helped me into my jacket. "Make it a thousand."

It leveled off at a hundred by the time we got my trench coat on, though I was happy for that. She offered to drive me home, but I told her I could make it.

"We can talk in the morning, then. After you've slept. Right now I want to call Justin's family in California."

I nodded. "He was tough. I doubt he told the kid anything."

"I'll let them know."

"And talk to Jerry."

"That, too. I'm determined." She stood on tiptoe and gave me a kiss. "You were great tonight." She turned and went off, the kilt swaying with her walk, the calves in her tanned swimmer's legs rippling. I watched her appreciatively. I'd take her over painkillers, any day.

Morrie the accountant offered to run me over to the lot where my car was parked, but I figured the fresh air would do me good. I said I'd muddle along okay.

32

AND MUDDLE IT was. When I got outside, a cold wind was grabbing everything handy and hurling most of it at me. My hat was probably halfway to Worcester. The moon had gone the color of ice. Whoever he was, the Old Farmer knew his stuff. When I got to my car and reached into my coat pocket for the keys, my fingers found something else.

I picked a route across the city. The walk to the car had wakened me briefly, but now I was fighting a thick tiredness, a yen to be in bed under a blanket of sleep, but I needed to answer a question while it was in my mind, before the pumpkins turned into coaches and took everything away. I found a booth near Kerouac Park and made a call.

As I drove up Mansur Street to the heights of Belvidere, leaves did a manic dance in the beam of the headlights. Behind and below me, in the distance, the city was a bewitched village, blurred by the morphine, without consequence now.

The turreted house on Belmont Avenue had the look of a sacked castle, the windows staring emptily. No candle-lit jack-o'-lanterns grinned from the stoop. I parked in the circular driveway. I was slow getting out, and when I did I spent another moment just holding on before I gimped to the door. Wind rattled the hemlocks. On my third salvo with the rampant-bear knocker, the fellow with the après-ski accent opened the door. I gave my name, in case he didn't recognize the disheveled figure in the trench coat standing there in the weak glow from the sconces. He didn't offer candy, but he was polite enough to let me step into the foyer of the grand hall. "It's late, sir," he said, frowning.

"You can say that again."

"Mr. Devlin has long since gone to bed."

His voice had an odd timbre in the big, shadowy room: Erich von Stroheim protecting Gloria Swanson in *Sunset Boulevard.*

"This is kind of important," I told him.

"It's all right, Heinz," said a voice from the dimness. "I couldn't sleep. Have Mr. Rasmussen come upstairs."

Heinz looked uncertain, but he knew who paid him. I walked slowly across the parquet and the oriental carpets to the winding staircase. I was tempted to ask to use the escalator chair, but that would have sounded silly. Anyway, the chair wasn't at the bottom. I climbed past the big paintings, pretending to admire them every few steps as I caught my breath. Basil Devlin stood at the summit, leaning on his dark cane. He was dressed in pajamas and slippers and a maroon satin robe, but that was the only color about him. He looked faded, his face pale, his fine white hair in disarray. Maybe he wanted me to feel at home.

"Come in," he said.

We went into the sitting room we'd been in that afternoon. The big fireplace stood empty and cold, the ashes swept out. Instead, a semicircle of quartz heaters buzzed and clicked thermostatically. Basil Devlin sat in one of the hard wooden chairs. "Thanks for seeing me," I said.

"Did you attend the show?"

"Enough. You heard what happened?"

"No."

Heinz came in. "I've brought your medication, sir."

It was some kind of green syrup, which Heinz poured into a spoon. The air in the room had a sweet, hospital smell. I missed the tart aroma of geraniums. I was glad for the quartz heaters, though. I could feel a draft moving down the chimney. Come winter, trying to keep this place warm would be a lost cause. When Heinz left, Devlin managed a weak smile. "My doctors warn me about pneumonia. Do you know what the old treatment for pneumonia used to be?"

I didn't.

"They'd bundle the patient under quilts and open the windows on a frigid night, on the theory that there are more molecules of oxygen in cold air. It was supposed to open the lungs."

"What's the new treatment?" I asked.

"I have no idea. I'm scheduled to fly to Palm Beach in the morning. I'm closing the house for winter. Doctors' orders. Are you all right?"

"Not bad," I said. "Got time for a story?"

"If it isn't too long. Heinz is right, I should be resting."

I sat down. I didn't waste time trying to find a fancy beginning. "Back in the early fifties, there was a fellow who taught drama at Harvard. And there was this right-wing group who felt his ideas were as red as Stanislavski. But Harvard isn't a place that worries a lot about that sort of thing. In fact, I gather it took pride in being on McCarthy's hit list. So this group figured another way to ruin the professor. He was married to the daughter of a prominent Back Bay family, and the group threatened to expose the fact that he was a closet bisexual. He told them to shove it, so they outed him."

"Outed?" Basil Devlin said.

"I know, it's one of the new words. Exposed him."

Devlin frowned.

"In the messiness, the man's marriage broke up, and for whatever reason, Harvard didn't renew his contract. He was blacklisted in his own way and was lucky to land a job at a little state teachers' school. In time he got married again, built a life. But later, when he saw a chance to exact some revenge on Harvard, by cheating in a quiz contest, I think he did."

"This is a curious ramble, Mr. Rasmussen, but you'll forgive me—I'm sure you didn't come here at this hour to tell me this."

"Sorry. It seems this professor did some research on the group that had tried to destroy him. He put it all in a journal. The group's had an interesting lineage over the years. The sons of slave traders, rumrunners, and later, right-wing politicos. Tom Chapman and son Paul bring it right up to date."

He looked at me in puzzlement. I was annoyed with this. "Come on, Mr. Devlin, it *is* late. Let's not jack each other up."

"Sir, I think you'd better leave."

He was right. In fact, if I'd felt stronger, I might have done just that. But my head was starting to swim again, and my face was hot. I loosened my tie and shifted position on the hard chair. "Tell me about Crossbones," I said.

The pale blue eyes had grown fierce. "I'm not asking anymore, I'm *ordering* you to leave."

"The Chapman kid was probably always was a bit rocky," I said. "High IQ, that talent for electronics, and Shakespeare too. But his father's death, and the revelation that his father was broke when he died pushed the kid over the edge. When I walked in here, and up to just a minute ago, my thinking was that though you condoned it, you didn't actually take part in what the kid was doing. I figured you may or may not have been guilty of anything criminal, but you'd certainly been party to stupidity. And since nobody else apparently has it figured, I wanted you to hear it."

"You don't know what you're talking about," Basil Devlin said, trying to work menace into his voice.

"Yeah, I do. Some of it. Paper spooks. Kooky letters to try to keep Corbin away. You played on the fact that the Chapman kid, like his father, was in Crossbones. Like you, and like all those Devlins there in the portraits. What was your ancestors' claim to membership? Founders of the Guy Fawkes society?"

"You're out of line."

"It happens. The kink in the hose was that Paul Chapman *wanted* Corbin here. He blamed Jerry for old crimes. Maybe he saw his own life jinxed before he was born, beginning that day Corbin and company beat his father's team, and his father got drunk with his teammates and boasted about how his club ought to take revenge. More likely he was just a sick kid whose old man had blown his inheritance and who needed someone to blame for things. Maybe *you* put him onto Corbin, got him the job working at the auditorium."

More of it was making sense now, coming in little flashes: like how Devlin had arranged for the fax and the private telephone in Corbin's hotel suite—installed by the Chapman kid, probably, who had used the phone bug to learn that Florence Murphy wanted to meet Chelsea in the locker room. Maybe he was afraid that she was going to tip Corbin that Westrake had cheated in the quiz bowl. The kid would have wanted that squashed because Corbin might start unraveling things, as *I* was trying to do. But my mind was struggling to hang onto the thread. Something like a stage curtain was descending slowly behind my eyes.

I moved forward on the chair, cleared my throat. "So the idea became to zap Corbin on live TV. I've got to assume you weren't doing it to impress Jodie Foster—so why? What did you need?" I fumbled the framed photograph out of my coat pocket, still talking, not wanting to lose momentum. "And then I got hold of it. I saw this and wondered, how does it fit? Who's this guy in the back here?"

Devlin's thickly veined hands clutched the picture of Chelsea's mother taken long ago, when she was a kid crooning songs for the sheer joy of it.

I went on, "A blind guy helped me see. I phoned Matty Silver on my way here just now. Seems you liked to go slumming down at Silver's jazz joint. He said you got to be a regular at the Canal Club—reserved table, bucket of champagne, and a corsage for the pretty singer."

Basil Devlin's eyes stayed on the photograph. "She was so beautiful," he murmured.

"Silver said you lost your heart to Betty Crown, only to lose her to a college kid whose folks were servants for your family. Big J was beating your time, and you . . . " I stopped, swallowed, started again. "You . . ."

It wasn't lockjaw, because that part worked fine: it was just that when I opened it, nothing came out. Devlin had lowered the old photo. He looked past me and nodded. And what came down on the back of my neck was no curtain. I jacked forward in the chair. I reached for something to take hold of, but there was nothing there.

33

THE SUN ROSE and set a hundred times, and old women slowly knitted a shroud. Above the click of their needles, I gradually grew aware of voices: muffled and distant, those of other inhabitants of the dark realm where I opened my eyes. There was a chill fall of moonlight on me. I was in a room laid out on the floor, alone. This was becoming a bad habit.

Then, with a faint metallic clinking, the sun began to rise again, and I squinted into the orange glow of a quartz heater coming to life. The warmth felt good. I lay there in it a long moment. The voices were still indistinct, but I realized now where I was and where the voices were coming from.

I counted fingers and recited my name. As feats go, it wasn't much, not like putting together a busy jigsaw puzzle; but that was already done. Now I just needed to bring in the cops. With great labor, I turned over onto my side and pushed to a sitting position. I worked my hand inside my coat and touched the bandage. Damp. I didn't look to see what color it was. A month later, I got my feet under me and stood up.

When I reached the doorway of the sitting room, where light from the hallway shone, I paused to consider the row of Devlin portraits. Each man smiled out at posterity, holding a book, now blue, now green; but always bearing the same little emblem that I had first seen on the book Paul Chapman had left behind at Harvard and had mistaken for a cross, but now knew represented a pair of crossed bones. I could almost hear the laughter of the painted faces. And the joke was on me.

At the head of the stairway, I thought for the second time that night that I'd like to use the escalator chair; and for the second time it was at the other end. Hanging onto the banister, I lowered myself a step. Then another. And another. I heard voices again. From below, beyond the turn in the stairs, one I didn't recognize said, "You're all set, sir. Everything's packed. The pilot's on his way to Hanscom Field now. He'll meet you there in an hour."

"All right. Now, listen carefully," Basil Devlin answered. "Once I've gone, I want you to contact the police. Speak with Lieutenant Droney. He may not be on duty, but insist that you speak with *him* personally. Tell him where you're calling from. Tell him you caught a prowler upstairs. He came at you abruptly, with a bloodstained coat, so God knows where he'd been or what he had in mind. But when he threatened you . . . was there a gun on him?"

"No, sir. Just the photograph, which you have."

"When he attacked you, you were forced to defend yourself. Have your bat handy. The police will want to know how he got banged up. You scuffled, and he fell down the stairs and broke his neck. It wasn't your fault. Do you hear what I'm saying?"

"Yes, sir."

"You got his name from the license you have there. Get that message to Droney. He knows Rasmussen was in trouble before and doesn't like him. He'll be interested in what happened."

"All right."

"Now go help Heinz load the luggage."

I felt the swirl of cold as the front door opened and closed. I reached the turn and could see down into the foyer. Basil Devlin sat in an ornate chair, facing away from me at an angle. He had changed out of his pajamas and robe and was wearing a topcoat and a cashmere muffler and a fur hat. His legs were wrapped in his plaid blanket.

I was ten feet from the bottom when the door opened again. A beech leaf skated across the parquet. A big man stepped in rubbing his hands together. He was wearing an Orioles batting helmet, and I recognized him as the Boog Powell look-alike who had been washing Devlin's Mercedes.

"Well, shit!" he said when he saw me.

Basil Devlin turned. The skin on his face tightened, and for a moment I could see how he had looked as an awkward and love-smitten man, out of his element with a working-class girl half his age who sang jazz. In a weary voice, he said, "Finish him, Gene."

Without a word the big guy reached into a corner behind a Chinese urn and produced a Louisville Slugger. He came across the foyer and started up the stairs. When he got to a point several steps below me, he swung. He didn't swing hard. I leaned back—not tough to do, since I was mostly falling—and just managed to hold myself up. The bat knocked a divot out of the wooden banister. I backed up another few steps.

Gene swung again, harder, and this time I did fall and sat down on the carpet runner as the bat fanned past my face. Getting up was hard labor. I backed up farther. My head had started to swim again.

The big guy climbed another step. He was playing with me, liking it, and probably would've backed me all the way to the top, but below, from his chair in the foyer, Devlin said, "Goddammit, hurry!"

Gene lifted the bat to his shoulder. Time to hit a homer. Gripping the railing as tightly as I could, I hiked myself up and kicked. My foot made the sound a fastball makes smacking a catcher's mitt. The big guy gave a wordless huff of breath. His eyes bugged. Then, arms pinwheeling, still clutching the bat, he fell backward. The helmet sprang away and he banged over every step, gaining momentum. At the bottom he somersaulted and caromed off the iron rail of the escalator chair and lay still. Devlin and I both stared, waiting. But I could see by the angle of the guy's thick neck that he wouldn't see another spring.

Ploddingly I started down the stairs. Devlin got up from his chair. The plaid blanket fell to the floor, and with it the portrait of Betty Crown. The glass in the art deco frame shattered. He stared down at the portrait a moment; then, slowly, he sank back into the chair.

"Time to call the cops," I said.

34

So Monday afternoon I drove them to the airport. Jerry Corbin sat in the backseat, dictating memos to an aide. Beside me in front Chelsea read aloud from the Boston newspaper accounts: " 'Aiding the efforts of Lowell Police was Private Investigator Alex Rasmussen, who a Jer-Cor publicist said was helpful in guaranteeing the television star's safety.' "

I caught Corbin's eye in the mirror. "Helpful?"

He laughed. "Well, you know how it is. There's a lot of fuzz and just one of you, and I suspect they watch a lot more TV." He bent forward and clapped my shoulder. "Hey, I made sure they spelled your name right."

Chelsea said, "They got it wrong."

"What're you talking?" Corbin took the newspaper. "I gave the reporter your card."

Chelsea looked at me and smiled.

"At least you got the cops to can the idea of yanking my license," I said. "That's worth plenty. Droney isn't my biggest fan."

"That guy. He's the kind of guy, you were a kid at scout camp, he'd come around in the night and take a leak on your campfire. I told him he could end up monologue fodder if he didn't shape up."

Earlier Corbin had met with Professor Westrake, and they

had forged a kind of peace. Gripaldi was still in the hospital, eagerly telling everyone who'd listen how it felt to get shot. The *Sun* was planning a feature on him. The videotaped *Gong Show* premiere had voluntarily been pulled from broadcast by Corbin, but the story of his heroism under fire was out and he was riding a wave of good press. The network had given a green light to do the series, and the first show was dedicated to the memory of Justin Ross. So things had worked out, kind of.

"Dev's case is a sad one," Corbin said. He had visited Basil Devlin at the Middlesex County jail. "Dev talked about the great ladder of being. How my family were shanty Irish and rightfully servants for his family because his had come over earlier and had made more money. But each successive wave of immigrants, he claims, has been less and less willing to assume its rightful rung, wanting to start at the top. It creates only disorder, he says, and according to him, I encourage it. I represent all of the media for him. Imagine. Kind of makes a fella proud."

I dropped them at their airline and went over to central parking, then hiked back to the concourse. When you're Jerry Corbin, you don't wait on airport lines. He and Chelsea were already in the departures corridor where the metal detectors stood. Jerry was surrounded by people in airline blazers, all laughing at a gag I missed. Probably the swami joke. When he'd shaken their hands and they'd gone, he waved me over. From a carry-on case he pulled out a dark blue beret. "A little gift," he said.

I looked at it. "How'd you know I wanted a fedora?"

He grinned and handed the beret to Chelsea. "That's for you, dear. You make a father proud." She put it on. She looked great. "And for you, amigo . . ."

It was a gray Stetson snap-brim, with a satin band and a little red cockade, an eighty-dollar job. I put it on and adjusted the brim. "Sharp," Jerry said.

"Definitely," Chelsea agreed.

"Pshaw," I said.

Corbin tugged his topcoat straight. "Okay. I'm not good at these things. Parting generally means I end up paying someone alimony. Though you've got some dough coming, too." He raised his hand to God.

"Whenever," I said.

He squeezed my hand. "You know you've always got friends in warm places. Come visit."

He went on through, wisecracking with the security people. He headed for the departure gates and didn't look back.

Chelsea said, "He likes you."

"Can you blame him?" I said. "Yeah. It's mutual."

"He'd love you to come out and take a job. He told me."

"I don't do well with earthquakes. Anyway, you two have got some catching up to do."

She lifted her eyebrows. "It's going to be interesting. I kind of wish you'd come, but I understand."

"This is my home turf. It don't take a shamus to see that the problems of three little people don't amount to a hill of beans in this crazy woild . . . "

Chelsea stood close to me. I could see her mother and her father in her features, and a whole lot more besides. Her eyes were as green and as moist as spring—except where I was going to be spring wasn't coming; winter was. I put my good arm around her and hugged her. She hugged back.

"Yowch!"

"Sorry. I forgot you're taped up."

We looked at each other for a long count, then she went down the sloped corridor after her father, stylish in her beret and long leather coat. She didn't look back, either. It ran in the family. I went outside and over to central parking, but I didn't get my car yet. I climbed to the roof deck.

Cold slashing rain had come in overnight, the spin-off from a storm over the Atlantic, stripping the last leaves from the trees and leaving the sky a deep, polished blue. In the distance, a V of Canada geese winged purposefully south. Autumn was gone. The Old Farmer said snow by Thanksgiving, and I believed him. I stood there in the chill November wind awhile, glad for the new hat. I watched planes grumble into the air. Maybe one of them was theirs.

I drove back through the tunnel and found a phonebooth in the North End and dialed the number for the Harvard Office of Alumni Affairs. When Judy Bishop answered, I said, "Who played Johnny Morrison in *The Blue Dahlia?*"

"Rasmussen."

"Close," I said. "It was Alan Ladd. I need some information."

She gave her throaty laugh. "Naturally. Go ahead."

"You doing anything later?"

"That's easy. No. Something else?"

I thought a moment and said, "You still like guys in hats?"